"Perhaps T̶... Explain Th̶... ...Walk Away From My Child."

"First things first. I need to confirm the pregnancy. Then we'll discuss the best way to handle the situation after that." She rose, the dame at her most grand. "Now, if you don't mind, I'd like to go home."

He did mind. He minded more than he could express.

Chase relaxed back against his chair and studied Emma, while making a swift analysis. She didn't work, mainly because she didn't have to. She'd been raised with a silver spoon in her mouth. And she was the last person he'd ever have chosen as mother to his child.

The irony didn't escape him. But unlike his father, Chase wouldn't allow Emma to give birth to a bastard, to force his son or daughter to deal with the sort of snobbery he'd dealt with his entire life. Whether she realized it or not, he was going to take control of both her and her pregnancy.

Starting now.

Dear Reader,

I have to say it's been an absolute pleasure being the launch author for Silhouette Desire's latest continuity series, The Takeover. This particular series is overflowing with hot, sexy, amazing characters and exciting plots, and is written by some of my favorite Desire authors. It's been wonderful working with them on this project.

One of my favorite parts of this story was the interaction between the various characters. I adored how the hero and heroine clashed over all that kept them apart, while moving from passion to a deep, unwavering love. I loved the way they came to terms with the heroine's pregnancy...*together.* And I really loved how they dealt with the various problem people in their lives in order to resolve the differences between them.

What could be better than reading about wonderful characters who find solutions to their problems and all the while discover something we all want in our own lives...the love of a lifetime!

Sit back, curl up with something hot and delicious (whether a beverage or a person—it's your choice!) and spend a few lovely hours falling in love. I thoroughly enjoyed writing this book and hope you'll enjoy reading it. Happy New Year!

Warmly,

Day Leclaire

DAY
LECLAIRE
CLAIMED: THE
PREGNANT HEIRESS

Silhouette
Desire

Published by Silhouette Books
America's Publisher of Contemporary Romance

Special thanks and acknowledgment to Day Leclaire
for her contribution to The Takeover miniseries.

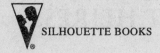 SILHOUETTE BOOKS

Recycling programs
for this product may
not exist in your area.

ISBN-13: 978-0-373-73073-5

CLAIMED: THE PREGNANT HEIRESS

Visit Silhouette Books at www.eHarlequin.com

Printed in U.S.A.

DAY LECLAIRE

USA TODAY bestselling author Day Leclaire is described by Harlequin Books as "one of our most popular writers ever!" Day's tremendous worldwide popularity has made her a member of Harlequin's "Five Star Club," with sales of well over five million books. She is a three-time winner of both a Colorado Award of Excellence and a Golden Quill Award. She's won *RT Book Reviews* Career Achievement and Love and Laughter Awards, a Holt Medallion and a Booksellers' Best Award. She has also received an impressive ten nominations for the prestigious Romance Writers of America's RITA® Award.

Day's romances touch the heart and make you care about her characters as much as she does. In Day's own words, "I adore writing romances, and can't think of a better way to spend each day." For more information, visit Day on her website, www.dayleclaire.com.

To Charles Griemsman, editor extraordinaire, who worked so long and hard on this project and added immensely to the concept. Thank you for everything you've done to put together such a fun and exciting series! It's been a true pleasure working with you.

One

She was here.

Chase stood in the shadows of the portico just outside the banquet room of the Vista del Mar Beach and Tennis Club. The room glittered and sparkled with both people and jewelry, the people in full cocktail-party mode, the jewelry, too, he supposed. Dead center in the middle of all that glitter and sparkle stood Emma, the woman he'd spent a single incredible night romancing, seducing...and then losing.

While dance music played in the background, voices rose and fell, determined laughter taking the edge off the rocky undercurrents that flowed around the room. Ostensibly the cocktail party celebrated the impending sale of Worth Industries to Chase's stepbrother and closest friend, Rafe Cameron. But old grudges and past secrets stirred restlessly beneath the surface. As his brother's money manager and one of those involved in negotiating the purchase of Worth, tonight marked the start of a rough and treacherous passage.

Chase studied Emma while he sipped a thirty-year-old

Laphroaig that his brother had stashed for those not interested
in the free-flowing champagne. The single-malt Scotch whiskey
went down as smooth as silk. Almost as smooth as Emma's
skin. She had a good portion of that skin on display, the pearl-
gray silk dress she wore clinging to curves he'd do just about
anything to uncover once again.

Her dress appeared vaguely Grecian in style, one shoulder
bared while the silk draped from the other shoulder across her
breasts. It hitched in a clever knot on her hip before flowing
to just beneath the knee. Continuing with the Grecian theme,
she wore toothpick-heeled sandals with straps that wrapped
around narrow ankles and trim calves. With her ice-blond hair
swept into an elegant chignon, she looked like a goddess. Like
a player.

His eyes narrowed. Which begged the question…what the
hell was she doing here? Since the guests were all connected
in one way or another to either Cameron Enterprises or Worth
Industries, she was, too. Either that, or she was the "plus one"
gilded on to a guest's invitation.

Maybe he'd wander over and find out. And maybe while he
was finding out, he'd ask her why the hell she disappeared the
way she had, leaving him ripping apart all of New York City
in a fruitless search for the mysterious Emma With No Last
Name. Before he could, Ronald Worth, soon-to-be ex-owner of
Worth Industries, joined Emma and placed a proprietary hand
on her bare shoulder.

Chase straightened, his mouth settling into a grim line.
No way. Surely she wasn't the arm candy of Rafe's nemesis.
Oh, hell, no. She couldn't possibly be sharing a bed with that
sixtysomething-year-old bastard. But based on the way good
ol' Ron lowered his head and whispered a loving comment in
her ear and the affectionate manner in which she leaned into
him and kissed his cheek, that was precisely what she was. Son
of a—

"Don't even think about it."

Chase glanced over his shoulder at the sound of Rafe's voice, his pale blond hair giving away his location in the darkness. "What?"

"The Princess. I see you staring at her, and I'm telling you. Don't even think about it. That one will eat you up and spit you out just for the sheer pleasure of it."

Chase fell silent, a tactic he'd learned during those rough, early years when he'd gone to live with his father. He turned to face his stepbrother, careful to conceal the anger surging through him. "You know her?" he asked mildly enough.

"Emma Worth, aka Spawn of Satan."

Chase lifted an eyebrow, relief replacing his anger. So she wasn't Ronald Worth's mistress, but his daughter. "I gather Worth is cast in the role of Satan?"

Rafe's grin lacked even a shred of humor. "What can I say? It comes naturally to him."

"And the daughter? What do you know about her?" Since Chase didn't want his brother to think he had a personal interest, he added, "Is she a factor in the sale?"

"She better not be a factor or she'll find herself moved out of the way by whatever means necessary," Rafe responded with characteristic ruthlessness. "But I don't think she'll be a player in any of this. She's shallow. Overindulged. Pure useless fluff."

"A party girl?"

Rafe hesitated. "A little lower profile than that. You don't see her plastered across the scandal sheets. More of a private party girl."

Chase turned and studied Emma once again while he considered this latest information. A private party girl. That fit with his experience, even though he hadn't picked up on the cues when they'd been together. Nor had she come off as shallow. But considering they'd only spent one night together, what the hell did he know?

More than anything he wanted to confront her, demand an explanation for her disappearing act. But perhaps he already had his answer, courtesy of Rafe. She was a party girl. One-night stands were as common to her as shopping for groceries was to the average woman. Even so, he hated being made a fool of, another throwback to his formative school years.

At the ripe age of ten, when he'd first arrived in New York to live with his father, Chase had been dubbed Barron's Bastard. That might have had something to do with the fact that his driven, world-renowned businessman father and his laid-back, California-mellow mother had never formalized their affair with traditional "I dos." He'd soon had the "California" knocked out of him by his peers at the private school where he'd been dumped and learned to keep his emotions and personal opinions under tight control. It was a lesson he never forgot and one that had helped propel him to the top of his field as a money manager.

His gaze narrowed on Emma in careful assessment. As Rafe suggested, she exuded wealth, privilege and glamour. From the elegant twist of her pale blond hair to the discreet glitter of diamonds at her earlobes and wrist, she sent out signals that mixed a sultry come-hither sexiness with an Ice-Princess touch-me-not facade. It all boiled down to one compelling objective. Chase wanted her with an unrelenting hunger. And one way or another, he'd have her again.

Tonight.

"How are you feeling, Dad?" Emma asked quietly, slipping her arm through her father's. "The party isn't too much, is it?"

"Don't fuss, sweetheart. I'm fine." Ronald Worth softened the testy edge in his voice with a smile. "It's a minor heart ailment, as you know damn well."

"Oh, really?" she challenged. "Apparently, it's bad enough to convince you to sell Worth Industries to Rafe Cameron."

He grimaced. "That's only one factor in my decision. I keep telling you, if you'd step in—"

"—which I won't, as I keep telling you."

"Well, there you have it. I could continue chugging along

for another decade or two." He glared down at her. "Don't give me that look, missy. I'm only in my mid-sixties. The prime of my life."

Emma smothered a smile. "I didn't say a word."

"You didn't have to."

She sighed, giving his arm a swift hug. "Are you sure you're doing the right thing? Even if running Worth isn't something I'd care to do, you don't have to sell if you'd rather not. You could delegate more. Hire someone to handle a greater portion of your day-to-day responsibilities."

"That's an option." Ronald's jaw firmed. "Selling is the one I chose instead."

"But selling to Rafe Cameron, of all people. From what little I've seen of him, he puts the *a* in arrogance."

His thick silver mane of hair glinting beneath the overhead lights, her father turned to glance in Rafe's direction. "Nothing wrong with arrogance when you have a solid pair of brass ones to back it up." A wistful note colored his words. "I was just like him at his age."

"Dad—"

"Enough, Emma. It's practically a done deal." Laser-sharp ocean-blue eyes gazed down at her and his harsh expression softened. "Have I told you how lovely you look this evening?"

She allowed her head to rest against his shoulder for a moment. "Just a chip off the old block."

He snagged her chin and tipped her face up to his. "You have all my best qualities and none of my worst. Same could be said about your mother. You have her staggering beauty but none of her weaknesses."

Emma's eyes misted. The fact that he'd mention her mother was startling enough. But for him to say anything positive about his late wife, even if it came across as a rather backhanded compliment, was downright shocking. Now if she could just get her father to reconcile with her brother. They weren't completely estranged. After all, her brother managed the family ranch at

Copper Run Ranch. But it had been more than a decade since the three of them had sat down like a family and talked to each other. Painful, irreversible events from the past prevented that from happening.

"Dad…"

He must have guessed the direction of her thoughts because he shook his head. "Forget it, princess. Not going to happen." He dropped a kiss on the tip of her nose. "Business calls. It's going to be a late night for me. Need to get out there and shake hands, kiss babies and steal lollipops. Will you be all right? If you want to leave early, you can take the car. Just send it back for me."

"Don't worry about me, Dad. I'll find my own way home." She gestured toward his executive assistant with a smile. "Kathleen's coming over. I'll ask her for a ride."

She could tell he'd already shifted gears. "Fine, fine. You do that. I have a few questions for William."

He made a beeline for Rafe Cameron's chief financial officer, William Tanner, a tall, gorgeous New Zealander who'd flown in for the party. He exuded a ruthless power similar to his employer's. Her father's departure left Emma standing alone, shaking her head. Not that she was alone for long. Kathleen Richards descended on her, snatching her up in an exuberant hug.

"Well, hello there, Emma. Aren't you a picture?" So was Kathleen. With her flaming red hair, bright green eyes and feisty personality, she never failed to light up the room, especially when dressed in eye-popping amethyst. "I swear, the only girl prettier than you is my granddaughter, Sarah."

Emma smiled, playing along. "Considering she's the image of you, that must make me the third prettiest girl."

Kathleen chuckled, the laugh unfettered and downright contagious. As always, heads swiveled in her direction at the trademark sound. "That's what I've always loved about you. You look upper crust, but you've always been real folk, same as that adorable brother of yours." She spared a swift look in

Ronald's direction and lowered her voice. "How's he doing, by the way? I swear I haven't seen him in a solid fifteen years."

"Neither have I. Since he decided to walk out on us, we—"

Emma broke off and inhaled sharply. No! It couldn't be. Of all the men in the entire world to show up out of the blue, Chase was the last one she'd ever expect to see. She'd spent every single day of the past two months trying to get this man out of her head, with zero success. And yet, there he was, walking toward her with the sleek, predatory prowl of a cougar, his ruffled blond hair the exact same golden-brown shade as a mountain cat's pelt.

"What's wrong?" Kathleen demanded. She glanced over her shoulder and chuckled. "Oh, I see. Let me tell you, Emma, I had the exact same reaction when Chase Larson walked into your dad's office. Took me a solid minute to find my jaw and pull it up off the floor. Tell you what. Why don't I introduce you?"

"No, you don't—"

She waved a hand at Chase. "Mr. Larson? I'd like to introduce you to Ronald's daughter, Emma."

"You don't have to—" Emma hastened to explain in an undertone. But it was too late to stop her. Far too late to stop him. "Chase and I have already met," she finished lamely.

"You've met?" Kathleen's gaze darted from one to the other and she grinned. "Well, then. Isn't that interesting. I'll tell you what. Why don't you two get reacquainted on the dance floor, while I get out of your way?"

"An excellent idea," Chase said. There was an unmistakable darkness edging his expression and lending a harshness to the deep timbre of his voice. He took her hand in his and gave a sharp tug, jerking her into his arms. He stared down at her, his blue eyes full of threat and promise. "Dance with me, Emma."

But all she heard was "Gotcha."

Chase took her in his arms, pulling her far too close. "Do you mind?" Emma attempted to ease back a precious few inches, only to have him tighten his grip. "In case you're unaware, breathing is a necessary component to dancing."

"If I don't hold you close you may run away again."

"I didn't run away before," she instantly denied.

She spared Chase a swift look, then wished she hadn't. At a smidge over six feet, he was an impressive man, his features attractively chiseled with a firm chin, strong, nicely shaped mouth and intelligent gray-blue eyes. She'd grown up around tough men and this was one more example of the breed, despite the patina of sophistication that cloaked him like a second skin.

When they'd met while flagging down a cab on that fateful November day the weekend before Thanksgiving, he'd been so charming that they'd ended up sharing the taxi. Granted, the charm had been rough-hewn and deliciously edgy. But that had only added to the romantic ambiance of the lovely fall weather. They'd ended up spending the entire day together, followed by the entire night.

Chase swung her around in an easy circle, his hand resting tantalizingly low on her back and sending frissons of temptation racing through her. "Funny. As I recall, you were there when I fell asleep and you were gone when I woke up. No goodbye kiss. No note. No way to find you."

Her brows drew together. "Then how did you?"

He gave a short, hard laugh. "You think I'm here for you?"

A hint of warmth drifted across her cheekbones. "I take it you're not," she said drily.

"I'm here to help finalize the Worth deal, Ms. Worth." He leaned on her last name. "Our meeting tonight is sheer coincidence since you didn't even bother to tell me who you were when we first met."

"I don't recall you asking. Nor do I recall you sharing your name at the time," she replied with impressive calm.

"Now you know it. It's Larson. Chase Larson." The name

rang a vague bell, but she couldn't quite place it. As though aware of that fact, he added, "I'm Rafe Cameron's brother."

She missed a step and Chase supported her weight while she recovered her footing. "Please tell me you're kidding."

"Problem?"

Where did she begin? Or perhaps she shouldn't begin at all. If Chase was anything like his brother, whatever she said would definitely be used against her. "Suffice to say the list is long and detailed." She focused on the knot of his crisp red bow tie, not daring to look at him in case her gaze reflected her distaste for his brother. "If you don't mind my asking, what's your involvement in the Worth Industries purchase?"

"I own Larson Investments, a financial investment firm. I'm helping Rafe put the purchase together."

No wonder his name sounded so familiar. She'd heard of Larson Investments. Who hadn't? That also meant that he was the illegitimate son of business tycoon, Tiberius Barron. Dismay filled her. How could her father possibly hope to negotiate a fair contract for the sale of Worth Industries when Rafe controlled such powerful factions? She moistened her lips. "I assume you're in favor of the deal?"

"Why wouldn't I be?" he replied, his expression giving nothing away. "Now that we've finished discussing our unexpected business connection, answer a personal question for me. That night we spent together, would you have told me your last name if I'd asked?"

Emma lifted a shoulder in a careless shrug. "I don't see why not." She glanced up at him and caught his guarded expression. "What about you? Would you have told me your last name?"

"Not our first night together."

She stiffened, offended. "I see. I'm supposed to be forthcoming with you, but—"

"I've discovered it's wise to protect myself."

"Protect yourself," she repeated, her eyes narrowing. "From what? Sexy little things who have an itch they're hoping you're rich enough to scratch?"

"Something like that." His gaze impaled her. "Are you a sexy little thing?"

How could she have found him charming? He wasn't the least bit charming. "Do you mean, am I after a wealthy husband or lover?"

"Are you?"

"No, thanks. You can relax. I have my own money."

"See?" He flashed a smile that was all too—yes—charming. "Now I've insulted you. It's not an easy question to ask on a first date, is it?"

She released a sigh. "Shall I assume that if I answered incorrectly when we first met there wouldn't have been a second date?"

"No, there would have been." Hunger flickered through his eyes so fast she wondered if she'd imagined it. "With you there definitely would have been."

She scanned his expression, understanding dawning. "But it would have come with strings. Or should I say, a lack of strings? You'd be willing to share my bed, but I'd better not get any ideas."

"Come on. Be fair, Emma," he chided. "Is it any different for you? Aren't you concerned that when men hear your name, learn of your connection to Worth Industries, they see you as their perfect shot at a life of leisure? To relax on a nearby beach sipping endless rounds of mai tais?"

Anger swept through her. "You give me far too much credit. Why would I object to that when it's clearly my goal in life, too? At least, that's your brother's opinion of me, something he's made abundantly clear the few times we've spoken."

"I believe that's because Rafe and I earned our fortunes the hard way."

"Whereas I inherited mine?"

She could tell him that she chose to devote her spare time to working at It's Time, the local women's shelter, but why should she be forced to defend herself when she'd done nothing wrong? Exhaustion swept over her worsening the headache, which had been gnawing at the edges of her consciousness all day. "Are we through here, Mr. Larson? I'd like to go home, if you don't mind."

"First, my brother's opinion does not reflect my own, so I'd appreciate it if you wouldn't color me with his brush. I prefer to form my own opinion about you, just as I expect you to form your own about me. And second, you still haven't answered my question."

She wondered if her desperation to escape showed. She'd had years of experience maintaining a calm, remote demeanor. But for some reason, whether the man or the occasion, she couldn't pull it off tonight. "What question?"

"Why did you leave without a word?"

She really didn't feel well. And now that she thought about it, it occurred to her that she hadn't eaten since breakfast. That, combined with the few sips of champagne she'd consumed, was leaving her seriously off-color. "Sorry, Chase, but we'll have to save this for another day." She pulled free of his arms. "You know who I am now and how to get in touch with me, assuming it's even necessary."

"What's wrong?"

"I haven't eaten," she admitted. "I'm feeling a bit light-headed."

She should have known better than to offer so much information to someone like Chase. He instantly took charge. "There's a buffet across the room. Why don't we find something that will help?"

She couldn't bring herself to look in that direction. Not when the scent of seafood drifted off the gleaming tables. "What I'd really like is to go home, put my feet up and fix myself some tea and toast."

"Fair enough. How did you get here?"

"With my father," she reluctantly admitted.

"You live with him?"

"Yes, but—"

"His estate is a few miles south of here, isn't it?"

She eyed Chase sharply. "How do you know that?"

"I get paid to know things like that." He cupped her elbow. "Come with me."

After collecting her wrap from the cloakroom, he drew her toward the wide-flung doors exiting onto the portico. A stunning view of beach and sea spread like a carpet beneath the bluff on which the Vista del Mar Beach and Tennis Club perched. A setting crescent moon dipped toward the Pacific Ocean, gilding the waves in silver.

He escorted her around the building toward the valet stand. "Where are we going?" she asked.

"You need tea, toast and quiet. That's what I plan to provide."

"What I need is to go home," she insisted gently.

And yet, somehow she found herself ensconced in the cherry-red Ferrari Fiorano Chase had rented. With the windows open, the chilly air helped clear her head. The instant he hit the freeway, he headed north, instead of south.

"Where are we going?" she asked, though at this point she wasn't sure she cared anymore.

"To get you something to eat."

Emma surrendered to the inevitable. She had a feeling that when it came to Chase there wasn't another option. Five minutes later he pulled in to a circular drive protected by an electronic gate and lined with palm trees. The instant he killed the engine, he helped her out of the car and escorted her to the front door of the beachfront condo.

"Is this yours?" she asked, impressed.

"Sorry to disappoint you, but it's a rental."

She wandered deeper into the condo. "This is gorgeous."

"I didn't bring you here so you could tour the place." He ushered her into the main living area, a huge room banked with floor-to-ceiling windows that overlooked the ocean. Stripping off his tux jacket, he slung it across the back of a chair. "Sit and relax. Tea and toast coming up."

As much as she wanted to insist that Chase take her home,

she didn't have the energy. She sank onto the couch and leaned against soft, thick cushions that molded themselves around her like a pair of warm arms. Despite all her attempts to remain alert, her eyes drifted closed. It wasn't until she heard the rattle of glassware that she opened her eyes again.

She glanced around, disoriented. "Did I fall asleep?"

"Just for a minute." He set a cup and saucer on a table at her elbow, followed by a plate with several slices of lightly buttered toast, cut into manageable bite-sized pieces. Pale greenish tea steamed gently from the clear glass cup. "Whoever stocks this place is big on herbal teas. This one's chamomile and peppermint. According to the package, it's guaranteed to relax and soothe."

"Thank you. Just what I wanted." Before she could take so much as a sip of tea her BlackBerry rang. She pulled it out of her purse and checked the caller ID. "Excuse me. I should take this. It's my dad."

The conversation was brief. But then, when it came to her father that was often the case. "Where are you?" he asked without preamble.

"With Chase Larson." She spared him a brief glance. "He offered to give me a ride home."

"Thought you were going with Kathleen."

"I changed my mind."

"Fine. Saw her here and I didn't see you, so I wondered."

She smiled, softening. "Thanks for worrying, Dad."

"Of course I worry," he retorted brusquely. "You're my little girl, even if you are all grown up. Good night, sweetheart. Don't stay out too late."

"'Night, Dad." She disconnected the call and dropped the BlackBerry on the table beside her tea and toast. She caught Chase's undisguised amusement and lifted an eyebrow. "What?"

He reached in his pocket and pulled out his BlackBerry. It was identical to her own. "I use the same ringtone, too," he said. "Great minds."

"I guess we'll have to be careful not to get them mixed up." She buried her nose in the delicate cup, inhaling the mild aroma. Then she forced herself to look at Chase. "Why are you doing this? I mean, why am I here? Why are you feeding me tea and toast instead of taking me home?"

He allowed his expression to say it all. "You know why."

She shook her head. "There's no point, Chase. You might be here long enough to put Rafe's deal together, but then that'll be the end of it. We live on opposite sides of the country. We want different things in life."

"How do you know that?"

She sighed and reached for a square of toast, nibbling on it. "Because I've met men like you before."

His eyes narrowed, the grayish-blue as turbulent as a stormy sea. "Men like me," he repeated softly, a disturbing tension rippling through his voice. "Would you care to explain what you mean by that?"

She took her time, finishing the slice of toast and washing it down with a sip of tea. She wanted to moan in pleasure, but didn't dare. Not when the gaze he turned on her still contained a whisper of desire mingled with a hint of intimidation. "Driven men. Men who put business ahead of everything else in their life. Men who live large and take whatever they want."

Amusement replaced his tension and, to her alarm, the whisper of desire became a shout. "What's wrong with taking what I want, especially if it gives you as much pleasure as it gives me?"

"Nothing. It makes—made—for an incredible night. But that's over now. I've returned to my life. You've returned to yours."

"And yet, here we are together again." He joined her on the couch, sitting far too close. "As long as I'm here, why not enjoy another incredible night or two?"

How did she answer that, explain the conflict over wanting a man so closely connected to Rafe Cameron? How did she explain she didn't want another incredible night? That getting over the first incredible night had been next to impossible? That if they spent another night together she might lose the final vestige of protection standing between her heart and her common sense?

She couldn't afford to fall for a man like Chase. She'd watched what living with a man like him—her father, to be exact—had done to her mother. It had destroyed her. Emma had taken the lesson to heart. What she and Chase experienced in November had been a lit match. Taking the next step might turn the affair into a dangerous wildfire, one that could consume and destroy instead of pleasure and warm.

She smiled, fighting to keep the moment light and easygoing. "Thanks so much for taking care of me, but it's time for me to go home. It's long past my bedtime."

"No problem."

Before she could guess his intention, he stood and swung her into his arms. "What are you doing?" she demanded in alarm.

"Since it's long past your bedtime, I'll see to it you turn in. Now." He carried her down a hallway and into a huge bedroom with views as spectacular as the living area. He released her so she dropped the few feet to the mattress. She bounced once before falling backward into the welcome embrace of the down-filled comforter. "And I'm turning in with you."

Two

She lay on the silk duvet in glorious disarray, outrage flashing across her gorgeous, Sleeping Beauty face. Between the breeze from the drive and her tumble onto his bed, her hair had escaped its intricate knot and long, loose curls fanned out around her head. Her eyes in the dimness of the room were hard to read. Her expression was not.

Color bloomed in her too-pale cheeks while indignation animated her face. "Have you lost your mind?"

He snagged the ends of his bow tie and yanked. "Not that I'm aware of." His shirt studs and cuff links followed and he dropped them carelessly onto the bedside table, followed by his BlackBerry. "I've wanted you back in my bed from the moment you left it."

She sat up. The light filtering from the hallway cut across the upper portion of her face, highlighting the incredible power of her eyes. The odd forget-me-not blue, a shade just shy of lavender, had haunted him for two endless months. Well, not any longer. Whatever it took, he'd find a way get her out of his system so he could continue his life without the memory of their time together distracting him.

"You can't believe I'm going to simply fall in bed with you."

"That's precisely what you did last time and what you're going to do right now." He stripped off his cummerbund and shirt, followed by his shoes. His hand dropped to the fastening of his trousers. "You feel it, Emma. Don't pretend you don't. It's gotten so strong that it hurts to breathe. I can't think about anything but you, about having you under me, being inside of you."

Her breath quickened and those eyes, those amazing eyes, darkened with raw passion. "I'm not some cheap one-night stand, damn it. I won't sleep with you tonight and have you walk away tomorrow."

Humor had his mouth curling upward. "I believe you were the one to walk away last time. And considering you don't have a car, I'm hoping you'll still be here when I wake up."

She waved that aside. "This is a mistake. You're part of Rafe Cameron's entourage." She inched toward the edge of the mattress. "I can't be seen fraternizing with the enemy."

That stopped him. Granted, there was no love lost between Rafe and Ronald Worth. But why would Emma consider Rafe the enemy? "Do you oppose the sale?" he asked softly. "Are you trying to stop it from happening?"

She led with her chin. "I'm not convinced your brother is the best person to run Worth Industries. There are too many questions about his future intentions that are still outstanding. But since it's not my decision, there's not much I can do about it, is there?"

"No, there isn't," he stated. Okay, warned her.

"But that doesn't mean I want to sleep with you. Not now that I know you're Rafe's brother."

"One has nothing to do with the other."

Her eyes narrowed in clear assessment. "How can I be certain you're not seducing me so I won't cause trouble?"

"First, because there's nothing you can do to stop the sale of Worth Industries to Rafe. It's as good as done. Second, when we made love that night in New York you were unaware of my connection to Rafe Cameron the same as I was unaware of your connection to Worth Industries." The sound of his pants zipper being lowered grated against the stillness in the room. "And finally, you know damn well that what we're experiencing tonight is identical to what happened two months ago."

"Except it isn't."

The instant she said the words her breath hitched and he knew she'd give anything to snatch them back. "No, it isn't," he agreed. He stripped off the last of his clothing and approached the bed. "This time it's far more intense."

She stared at him, riveted. He waited to see whether she'd attempt to evade him, but to his surprise she didn't. One minute she sat on the edge of the bed and the next she came into his arms. The silk of her dress flowed across his flesh like a teasing caress, while the curves that lay beneath it impacted against him, warm and delicate and deliciously feminine.

"This is a mistake," she informed him.

He could barely contain his groan. "How can it be when we feel like this whenever we touch?"

He scorched a pathway of fire along her bared shoulder to her neck. Cupping the back of her head, he drew her up for a kiss. A low, delicious moan escaped her and her lips parted, surrendering beneath his. She tasted amazing. How had he survived two whole months without tasting her again? Without having her in his arms. And soon—very, very soon—he'd have her beneath him, be inside of her again. One way or another, before he left Vista del Mar, he'd quench the insatiable thirst she roused in him.

He pulled back and smiled down at her. "You're overdressed, sweetheart."

"Oh, I don't know." She offered a swift, gamine-like grin. "I rather like having you naked and at my mercy."

"And what do you plan to do with me?"

"This…"

Her hands slid downward, over steely abs, and lower still. She cupped him, her hands unbelievably soft, shaping the length and breadth of him with gentle strokes. He almost lost it. But when he attempted to pull away, she shook her head in mock disapproval.

"Ah, ah, ah. You're at my mercy, remember?"

Hell. "Is there any point in begging you to be gentle with me?"

"None." A sultry smile drifted across her mouth and deepened the color of her eyes. "Since you're one of those types who likes to be in charge all the time, you have to play this my way or we don't play at all."

"I'm not sure I like those rules," he complained.

Just when he thought he couldn't control himself a moment longer, she slid her hands upward and wrapped them around his neck. "But you'll play by them, won't you?"

He shot her a look filled with a combination of threat and warning. "For now."

She tilted her head to one side in assessment. "Something tells me you're a dangerous man to cross," she said slowly.

"That something is called sheer self-preservation. I'd listen to your instincts."

She simply laughed. "You wouldn't hurt me."

"How can you possibly know that? We've only been together for a handful of hours."

Her laughter faded beneath the challenge of his statement and she studied him, pinned him in place with a penetrating stare. In that moment, he could see the father reflected in the daughter, the same fierce determination. "Is that the sort of man you are? Do you deliberately try and hurt people?"

"No. Not even a little. Will I hurt you? I hope like hell I won't. It depends on where this takes us and what we decide to do about it if we continue down this road."

A shadow flickered across her face. "I don't want to worry

about what happens next. If we're going to do this, I can only handle tonight."

"Then let's make tonight count," he suggested, allowing her a glimpse of the intensity of his passion.

She teetered, but she'd already made her decision, had made it shortly after he'd dumped her on to the bed. Whatever they'd ignited in his penthouse apartment in New York had continued to burn, the embers buried but still white-hot and ready to burst into flames with a simple touch.

"Please make love to me," she whispered into the darkness.

"My pleasure."

She pulled him in for another kiss, this one slow and languid, expressing a longing that matched his own. "Undress me," came the hungry command.

"I was hoping you'd say that."

He found the zip beneath her arm and lowered it. The bodice loosened, parted, allowing him access to the soft roundness of her breast. He shaped it in his hand and felt the nipple tighten and swell. She was so elegantly made, delicate and fine-boned. And yet there was a supple strength beneath her softness that spoke of someone well-honed in both body and spirit.

He pulled her up off the bed and into his arms, allowing the gown to drift downward. It snagged at the swell of her hips and she gave a quick shimmy that sent it sliding to the floor. She stood before him clad in garter and stockings, a small pale triangle of silk panties protecting her modesty. He eased her back onto the mattress.

"You're beautiful, Emma."

The words seemed so inadequate. Shallow. And despite what Rafe claimed, Chase didn't find anything shallow about Emma. Granted, he didn't know her well. Yet. But her intelligence glittered in her eyes, and enthusiasm exuded from her, a quiet, wholehearted joie de vivre filling her up and overflowing onto everyone around her.

With swift, economical movements he loosened the straps of

her heels and tossed them aside. He took more time removing her
garters and stockings, tripping his fingers along the outer edge
of her shapely legs and then up again along the sensitive inner
length. She shivered when he reached her thighs. Moaned as
he approached the apex. Released a soft cry of need the instant
he cupped the very heart of her through her silk panties.

Just that one touch left her teetering on the brink, as
close to going over as he was. At the last possible moment
he remembered to grab a condom from the nightstand table.
Then he swept her panties from her hips and settled down on
top of her. Her lips were swollen from his kisses and a flush
ran feverishly high along the curve of her cheekbones. Passion
turned her eyes dark with need, a ripe, blistering ardor that
more than matched his own.

"Why did you leave me last November when we have this
between us? When it only takes a single touch for us both to
go up in flames?" he demanded. "Why didn't you tell me who
you were or how to find you again?"

"I was afraid."

"Afraid of me?"

She shook her head, her hair forming a pale, tangled halo
of white gold. "Not of you. Never of you. I was afraid of this.
Of wanting someone like you so much."

"Afraid of how you respond when we come together?"

In one swift move he mated their bodies, one to the other.
The breath sobbed from her lungs. "Yes. Oh, please don't stop.
I've been waiting so long to feel like this again."

"Look at me, Emma. I want you to know who you're
with."

Anger burned alongside her desperation. "I know who I'm
with, Chase. How could I possibly forget how it was between
us?"

The admission threw him off stride, but only for a moment.
"It'll be even better this time," he promised.

Because this time he knew what she wanted. What made
her sing. What made her explode. What made her soar within

his arms. And he'd do everything within his power to give her all that and more.

As much as he wanted to take her fast and hard, he wouldn't. Couldn't. He needed that slow build, to experience that climb every inch of the way. To absorb her breathless moans with his every kiss and have that soft, soft flesh brushing against his. To savor the sweet scent of desire gathering in the air and taste it on her mouth and skin.

He sampled first her lips, then her breasts. And he moved with her, a slow, gliding waltz. He caught her hands in his and locked them over her head, their fingers entwined. Her legs slid along his, her toes pressing into his calves in joyous welcome, then wrapping around his hips, anchoring him tight. The tempo increased, moving from waltz to tango.

Sighs turned to murmurs of demand. Control escaped his grasp. How was that possible? He never lost control with women. Always maintained a safe distance even in the most intimate of situations. Never allowed anyone to glimpse his raw emotions in case they were used against him. But with Emma... The dance grew ever faster and he surrendered to the drive, to the magical music the two of them made whenever they came together. She arched beneath him, bowing upward as her climax slammed through her. He couldn't help himself. He followed her up and over, leaping with her into that glittering place of rapture met and fantasy realized.

Silence reigned for endless seconds afterward, while they both struggled to catch their breath. "How do you do that?" Emma asked at last, gasping for air. "How do you take us so much further than I ever believed possible?"

Her heartbeat thundered against his, a perfect counterpoint to his own. "It's a skill."

"One you have down pat, apparently." She spared him a speaking glance. "Lots of practice?"

"Some. But with you—" He broke off before he revealed too much.

"With me...what?"

"It's different." And that's all he intended to say.

She slipped out from beneath him and curled tight against his side, one leg thrown across his. "Different how?"

How the hell had he gotten into this? He decided to take the manly way out. "Why ruin the moment by picking it apart?"

She simply laughed. "Oh, please. You can't get out of explaining yourself with that old dodge. You're the one who brought it up."

"You know it's different without my explaining how or why," he insisted gruffly.

"I just wanted to hear you admit it." She relaxed against him. "And if it makes you feel any better, I don't understand why we're like this together, either."

Chase had always been good at analyzing disparate elements and organizing them into a recognizable shape. It was one of the factors that made him such an outstanding investor. The instant Emma admitted that her reaction to him didn't mirror what she experienced with other men, a puzzle piece clicked into place, causing that night in New York to assume a new and fascinating shape.

"You realized it the first time we were together, didn't you?" he asked. "You realized that what we feel when we're together is different somehow."

She reluctantly nodded. "Yes."

He dropped the other shoe. Hell, a closet full of shoes. "And that knowledge scared you."

She hesitated for another telling moment before asking, "Doesn't it scare you?"

"Anything I can't control scares me," he admitted.

"So what now?"

"Now we go to sleep."

She didn't speak for a brief moment, then remarked, "Wait until the cold light of day when we're both running scared before discussing what happens next?"

His mouth twitched. Her sense of humor always took him by surprise. It was something he was learning to appreciate about her. "Better than making rash or stupid decisions in the post-heat of passion."

"Okay."

He slid his fingers into her hair and turned her toward him. "You're still going to be here when morning comes, right?"

"As you pointed out, I don't have a car. Plus, you know where I live." She gave an exaggerated shiver. "I'd just as soon you not come pounding on my father's front door demanding to know why I'm not still in your bed."

"Fair enough. Tomorrow we'll discuss this rationally over breakfast like two mature adults."

Chase woke to an empty bed and shot upright. Son of a bitch! So much for discussing their situation like two mature adults. He touched the sheet beside him, expecting to find it stone cold. To his relief it was still warm, which meant Emma couldn't have gotten far. He escaped the bed, and almost tripped over her dress. It rested in the middle of the floor in a crumpled pearl-gray heap of silk where he vaguely remembered tossing it.

He checked the nightstand table for his car keys. They were there, right beside his BlackBerry. Okay. Chances were Emma hadn't taken off naked and hitchhiked home. That meant she was around here, someplace. He noticed the bathroom door was closed and smiled.

Gotcha.

He padded across the room naked and rapped lightly on the door. "Why don't I get the coffee going?" he offered.

"Fine."

Chase paused. Her voice sounded odd, tight and almost pained. "You okay?"

"Fine."

There it was again, that underlying edge of despair. It didn't take much thought to figure out what caused it. Morning-After Regret. Well, tough. She'd have to deal with it because he didn't regret what happened one little bit. And he intended it to happen again at their earliest convenience…like immediately after breakfast.

He snagged a pair of jeans and yanked them on before heading toward the kitchen. At the last second he pocketed the car keys, just to be on the safe side. He wished he'd remembered to add beans and water to the coffeemaker last night. If he had he'd be enjoying his first hit of caffeine right this minute—the most crucial part of his morning—instead of waiting the endless five minutes it would take to percolate.

But he'd had more important matters on his mind the previous evening. Like Emma. He made short work of the coffee and opened the refrigerator to rummage through the contents, not that it offered up much in the way of real food. He spent most mealtimes in a restaurant entertaining clients or, occasionally, a woman. So what did he have that qualified as breakfast?

Beer. Okay, he considered that real food, at least it was in his world. Still, probably not the best option to offer Emma for breakfast. He shoved the beer aside and pulled out a carton of eggs. That would work. Bread and butter. He still had some left over from last night. And a pint of half-and-half. Fair enough, he decided. It could be worse.

He consumed his first cup of coffee while making some halfway decent scrambled eggs, even if they were a tad rubbery, and toast that wasn't too badly burnt. After dumping everything onto two plates and placing them on the breakfast table, he poured a second cup of coffee for himself and a first one for Emma. Based on what she'd ordered after their one dinner together, she liked it heavy on the milk and light on the sugar. Considering he spent his day putting together million-dollar deals and handling tens of millions worth of investments, he was inordinately pleased with himself over throwing together such a simple breakfast. Now he just needed someone to share it with him.

"Emma?"

He entered the bedroom, his brows snapping together when he saw that she still occupied the bathroom. No sound of running water. No feminine splashing or fussing. Just a nerve-wracking silence. Hell. She'd been off-color last night. Was she sick? He tapped on the door.

"Sweetheart? Are you all right?"

"Go away," she moaned.

"The hell I will. Fair warning, I'm coming in."

"No, don't—"

"Too late. I'm in."

To his concern, he found Emma curled up on the tile floor, her face buried in the knees she'd drawn to her chest. He'd have found it amusing that she wore his dress shirt from the night before if she didn't look so utterly wretched. He crouched down beside her and smoothed her damp hair away from her brow. Her complexion was as snowy white as his shirt, with just the merest hint of green for contrast. Not a good color combination on her.

"I'm sorry, Emma," he said sympathetically. "I didn't realize you were unwell. What can I do to help?"

"Other than go away?"

He smiled. "Sorry, sweetheart, I'm not made like that. What's option number two?"

"Hold my head while I get sick again?"

He winced. "Stomach virus? Food poisoning?"

"That would be nice," she replied in a muffled voice.

Okay, that didn't make the least bit of sense. "Why would a stomach virus or food poisoning be nice?" he asked cautiously.

She lifted her head, her eyes dark and bleak. "Think it through, Chase. You'll get there."

Maybe if he'd downed that second cup of coffee it would all make perfect sense to him. After all, his analytical skills were pretty damn impressive. But for some reason they seemed to be on the fritz this morning. He shook his head, indicating his bewilderment. "I'm obviously missing something here. Care to fill me in so we can both be on the same page?"

She sighed. "Take one woman. Add a tablespoon of gee-she's-sick. Toss in a cup of second-missed-period." She made a small stirring motion with her finger. "Mix with hey-it's-morning. And guess what you get?"

No. Oh, hell no. "You're pregnant?" He meant to ask the question calmly, with the same stony cool attitude with which he'd learned to handle all of life's crises. Unfortunately, somewhere between "you're" and "pregnant" his voice had risen to a roar.

She flinched. "I don't know for certain. But I'd say all the signs are there."

"You said…" He shot a hand through his hair, struggling to think straight. What the devil had she said? "You said second missed period. As in January, minus two equals November. We were together in November. We were together, together in November."

"You know something, Larson?" she asked, an edge in her voice. "You really are a genius when it comes to numbers and statistical analysis."

"Can the sarcasm, Worth. I'm not the one on the floor puking my guts out. As I recall we used protection each time we made love that night." He never, ever made love without precautions, since he'd never risk the possibility of history repeating itself.

"Yeah, that bothered me at first, too." To his horror tears filled her eyes. Huge, gut-wrenching, I-can't-believe-this-is-happening tears. "It was the shower that did us in."

"The shower," he repeated stupidly.

"Exactly. The shower. It came off, remember?"

He winced. That's right. It had. "You think the baby's mine?"

"No," she shot back, insulted. "The baby's mine. You were simply involved in the conception."

He bit off a sharp retort. Sniping wouldn't get them anywhere fast. First things first. "Have you seen a doctor? Had a pregnancy test?"

She closed her eyes and shook her head. "I've been deluding myself the past few weeks that I was simply late."

"Two months late?"

"It happens," she retorted defensively. "Or so I've heard. But now…"

"Now you're not so sure."

She buried her face in her knees again. "No."

He struggled to think logically, to tackle the problem—assuming a baby could be considered a problem—one step at a time. "First, is there anything I can do to help with the sickness?"

"Tea and crackers would be nice."

"I have the tea, but not the crackers. But since I'm going to run out to a pharmacy and pick up a pregnancy test, I can snag some crackers at the same time. I assume you want plain versus fancy? Crackers, that is."

She shuddered. "Very plain."

"Emma?" He waited until she lifted her head and looked at him. "One way or another we'll figure this out. First on the list is to find out whether or not you're pregnant."

A hint of amusement brought some much-needed color into her face. "There's a list already?"

He leaned in and kissed her forehead. "Honey, there's always a list."

Chase soon discovered the difficulty wasn't finding a pregnancy test. It was choosing among the dozen options that filled the shelves. Finally, he simplified matters and scooped up one of each before heading for the checkout counter. The cashier gave him an odd look.

"That hopeful or that afraid?"

He could hear Brooklyn in her voice, a familiar whiff of home. Chase handed over his card and gave her a steely look that had successfully cowed some of the toughest businessmen New York had to offer.

"Charge it," he told her.

For some reason The Look didn't work with Brooklyn. "I'm just saying."

Fortunately, the crackers and the basketful of basic food groups he decided he should add to his ever growing list proved far less stressful to purchase at the grocery store. This cashier, clearly a native Californian, limited himself to a polite "Have a nice day." And though he didn't actually say "dude," it was implicit in his voice. Considering that he'd been born and raised here in Vista del Mar, before going to live in New York with his father at the tender age of ten, he had feet planted on both coasts. Memories cascaded through him of a life he'd given up all those years before. Carefree years. Lean years. Years filled with laughter and a mother who adored him. He shoved the bittersweet images aside, refusing to dwell on the what-ifs if he'd made a different choice and forced himself to maintain his focus on the job at hand.

Chase returned to the condo, collecting a speeding ticket along the way. Officer Garcia was also excruciatingly polite and Chase made an executive decision to avoid choosing a red Ferrari for his next visit. You just couldn't go wrong with basic black. He found Emma where he'd left her and joined her on the floor, upending the bag from the pharmacy.

Emma stared at the dozen boxes. "I appreciate your enthusiasm, but I don't have this much pee."

"I didn't mean for you to use all of them." Though if the first result proved positive...or negative... Chase frowned. Proved baby-on-board, he'd insist she take another one. "I figured you could choose the easiest to use."

"I think they're all pretty much the same. But maybe some are easier to read than others."

"Right. Start with those."

She lifted an eyebrow. "Start?" When he didn't say anything, she sighed and pointed to the door. "If you don't mind, I'd rather do this in private."

He stood and stared down at her. She looked so small and delicate, curled up on the floor. "You'll call me as soon as you know anything?"

"Of course."

"And, Emma...?"

She spared him a swift glance, but didn't speak.

"If the baby's mine, I'll do the right thing," he informed her. "For both you and the child."

And with that, he left.

Three

For several minutes after Chase exited the bathroom, Emma didn't move. Then, reluctantly, she lined up the boxes along the spotless counter before sinking back down onto the equally spotless tile floor. She stared at them. They stared back, whispering to each other, no doubt talking about her and her situation.

Pregnant.

Emma splayed her fingers over her abdomen. Was she? She suspected it was all too likely. For weeks now she'd made excuse after excuse to explain away the telltale symptoms, first because she had no idea how to find Chase. And second because she dreaded the coming confrontation with her father when she informed him of her condition.

The boxes continued whispering, and with an exclamation of annoyance, she snatched the first of the pregnancy tests off the counter—the noisiest of the twelve—and ripped it open. She scanned the literature, determined to get the test over with as soon as possible. Maybe then the boxes would shut up and leave her alone.

The directions informed her that it only took *One Minute!* to obtain the results. *Just Sixty Seconds!!*—for those who needed further clarification as to the meaning of a minute. The directions didn't lie. As promised, precisely *One Minute!* later she had her answer. Stripping off Chase's dress shirt, she stumbled into the shower and stood beneath the pounding spray struggling to keep from hyperventilating.

How odd that in *Just Sixty Seconds!!* her life could change so dramatically. From *One Minute!* to the next she went from being an average healthy woman to someone carrying the spark of new life. She snatched a deep breath. Okay, it wasn't the end of the world, not even close. It simply confirmed what she already suspected in her heart. She could deal with this, she told herself. Sure she could.

Sometimes life brought her to her knees with a blow so hard she didn't think she could endure it. But she always fought her way back. She always came out swinging. She always triumphed. She'd handled far worse events during the past twenty-five years—the death of her mother, for one—and managed to survive the ordeal. She blinked against the painful burning in her eyes. She would on this occasion, too. Plus, a baby wasn't a death to grieve or some horrible disaster, but a life to celebrate, even if unplanned.

Another possibility struck. Tests like these weren't always accurate. Lots of times they gave off false readings. What if this was one of those times? What if she'd read the directions wrong or hadn't followed them correctly? She'd been in a hurry. It could have happened. She turned off the water, grabbed one of Chase's large, fluffy towels from the built-in linen closet beside the tiled shower stall and wrapped it around herself. This time she'd read everything twice. Be meticulous. Make sure she followed the instructions exactly.

Thirty minutes later she stood in front of the bathroom sink, one lined with a full dozen little sticks and wands and trays with circular windows. She clutched the stack of instructions for each of the tests while she went down the row, comparing picture to actuality.

Two pink lines. Pregnant.

A plus mark. Pregnant.

Little window that actually spelled out *pregnant.*

Another little window that had forgotten the *not* in front of that all-important word.

Two blue lines. Very pregnant.

On down the row she went until she reached the very last tray. They all said the same thing. The little windows glared up at her with their little lines and crosses and plus marks and those *P* words. She backed away from them until she hit the wall next to the shower stall and sank back onto the bathroom floor. She should be horrified. She should be terrified. In a panic. Her brows drew together. Why wasn't she in a panic?

Her hand stole across her abdomen. She was pregnant. Her baby grew here, nestled deep within her womb. Hers and Chase's. She wasn't panicked, she realized, any more than she was horrified or terrified. A child. Dear heaven, she'd been given a child. She'd been given the chance to have a family again, one not torn apart by death and disaster, dishonesty and despair. The tears came then, but to her amazement, she discovered they weren't tears of misery or fear.

They were tears of wonder.

Chase frowned at the bathroom door, a firmly closed bathroom door. How long did a simple pregnancy test take, anyway? He thought he'd seen one of the packages exclaiming: *Response in just one minute!* Maybe she hadn't used that one. Maybe she'd used the one that read: *Response whenever we damn well want to give it to you!*

Unable to wait another second, he tapped on the door. "Emma? Do you need help?" He shut his eyes. Help? That was wrong on every possible level. "I have your tea and crackers."

Of course, the tea was now iced tea and the crackers were probably stale. The hell with it. "Emma, I'm coming in."

He found her more or less where he left her, curled up on the floor. Only now she wore a towel instead of his shirt. He couldn't decide if that was a good sign or a bad one. She looked up when he entered and waved a slim hand in the direction of the counter.

"Take a look," she said.

To his surprise, she'd used all twelve tests. "No wonder it's taken you so long. How much water did you have to drink to pull this off?"

"Think camel and add a gallon or two."

"So, what's the verdict." He examined the lineup and stiffened. "Some of these say pregnant."

"All of them say pregnant."

"All?"

He whipped around, feeling sucker punched. Until that moment he'd refused to consider the possibility that she might actually be pregnant, had maintained an emotional distance from the unfolding events. He'd managed to convince himself that Emma had made an understandable mistake, one rectified by a simple test. After all, why stress until there was something to stress about? Well, there sure as hell was something to stress about now.

"All?" he repeated.

"Every last one. Look, I'd rather not discuss this dressed in a towel, if you don't mind," Emma said in an excruciatingly polite tone of voice. She pushed herself upward. "I need to get dressed."

His brain switched to automatic, processing and stringing words together in a seemingly calm and coherent manner. "You can wear your dress from last night, although it's pretty wrinkled. Or I have a T-shirt and running shorts you can borrow."

"Thank you. I think the tee and shorts would be more comfortable."

He realized he blocked her exit and stepped back into the bedroom. Emma trailed after him. Still moving on automatic pilot—dear God, a baby—he opened a dresser drawer, retrieved the promised clothes and set them on the bed.

He gave her a searching glance. She remained ghost-pale, though not as shell-shocked as he undoubtedly looked. In fact, her poise impressed the hell out of him. "We need to talk," he announced.

"In all honesty, I'd rather go home. Perhaps we can meet in a few days and discuss the situation then. That will give us time to assimilate the information."

Assimilate the information? What was he, a Borg? He'd already assimilated all he needed to know. Emma was pregnant and she'd pasted a big, fat red arrow over his head, labeled Daddy. Still, it wasn't worth arguing with her, not when she didn't feel well. Since she couldn't go home without his driving her there, she couldn't very well control what he chose to say or discuss between now and then. Nor would he allow her to leave without feeding her first. Feeding their child. He shot a hand through his hair. Aw, hell.

"Get dressed, sweetheart. I'll freshen up your tea and crackers."

"Thanks. I'm actually starting to feel a little hungry."

She joined him a short time later and he smiled at the droop of his running shorts on her daintier frame, while something visceral swept through him at the sight of her breasts outlined by the thin cotton of his T-shirt. Were they larger due to the pregnancy, or was it his imagination?

"Since you said you were hungry, I opened up a very mild bean dip to go with the crackers, if you want. Or, if you're in the mood for eggs, I can scramble up some more."

"More?"

He shrugged. "I made some earlier. The trashcan says thank you."

She smiled at that. "Believe it or not, the bean dip sounds great. Do you have any fruit?"

Good thing he'd decided to pick up a few of the basic necessities from each food group. Even better, he actually considered fruit a food group. "In the fridge."

She pulled out an orange and proceeded to strip away the rind and section it, then went back for a kiwi and some black grapes. Satisfied with her selection, she arranged the dip, crackers and fruit onto plates, her artistry impressing the hell out of him. Then, with uncanny accuracy she crossed to the cupboard that contained place mats and linen napkins and proceeded to set the table with the same style and eye appeal.

"Okay, how do you do that?" he demanded.

Her smile grew. "Years of practice entertaining my father's clients. My mother—" She faltered for a split second before continuing. "My mother was an artist. I guess I inherited her eye for color and space."

"Do you paint?"

Emma took a seat at one of the chairs surrounding the glass breakfast table and waved him to the one opposite her. "Not so much as a brush stroke." She unfolded the napkin and placed it in her lap. Even when enjoying a casual breakfast dressed in his running clothes, she exuded a natural elegance in the way she sat and moved. "I'm lucky if I can draw a straight line."

"But you wish you could draw," he guessed shrewdly.

She nibbled on a cracker smeared with bean dip. "You're right. I do."

"Maybe our baby will inherit her abilities," he said, deliberately introducing the subject of Emma's pregnancy.

"Let's hope that's all he or she inherits," Emma murmured.

His gaze sharpened and he made a mental note to research Ronald's late wife. Chase vaguely remembered some sort of scandal from his youth, but couldn't quite recall the details. It must have been after he'd moved to New York to live with his father. He didn't think his mother had ever mentioned it, though she hadn't moved in the same circles as the Worths then—or now.

"Fair enough. You don't want certain characteristics of your mother to show up, and I have to admit there are a few anomalies I'd just as soon any son or daughter of mine didn't chip off the old genetic block." He paused, then asked, "Should I assume you plan to keep the baby?"

"That's the only part of this you can assume. I will have the baby and I'm not considering adoption. I…" She caught her lower lip between her teeth. "I couldn't. I couldn't give my baby away."

"Our baby. At least, I assume it's ours." He wished there were a less awkward way of asking his next question. "You implied I'm the father."

"There's no other possibility." She made the statement with calm certainty.

"You're sure?"

She jabbed an orange slice in his direction. "All right, Money Man. Let's put this in terms even you can understand. One woman who's had a rather lengthy sexual dry spell plus one man who ended aforementioned dry spell, minus one condom equals oops. In case you missed it, I double-checked my math twelve different times. It came up baby on every test."

He would have laughed if the situation weren't so serious. "I'm not questioning your math."

Her expression froze over. "You're just questioning which of my many lovers is the father, is that it?"

He cautiously moved the question aside and out of reach. "I assume you won't object to a paternity test?" he asked instead.

"Of course not."

"In utero?"

Her brows drew together. "They do that now?"

How the hell should he know? He'd never been in this situation before. Had done everything within his power to prevent it from ever happening. "We can ask your doctor."

Emma shoved her plate aside. "There is no *we*."

"If there's a baby, there sure as hell is a *we*." He leaned forward to give emphasis to his words. "Perhaps this is a good time to explain that I won't walk away from my child. If it's mine, I'll be intimately involved every step of the way."

"First things first. I—and I do mean I—go to see my ob/gyn and confirm the pregnancy. Then we'll discuss the best way to handle the situation after that." She rose, the dame at her most grand. "Now, if you don't mind, I'd like to go home."

He did mind. He minded more than he could express. But he hadn't gotten where he was in the world by losing his temper or indulging in a knee-jerk reaction when someone gave him a verbal shove. Chase relaxed back against his chair and studied Emma, while making a swift analysis. She was beautiful and clever and fascinating. But, she was also a Worth, which meant she came from money. Unfortunately, that small detail made her the last person he'd have chosen as mother to his child because he'd had so many bad experiences with others who came from that rarified world of inherited wealth.

The irony didn't escape him. No doubt his father had felt the same dismay when Penny Larson had informed him of her unplanned pregnancy though Tiberius Barron's reasons would have been far different. Unlike his father, Chase wouldn't allow Emma to give birth to a bastard, to force his son or daughter to deal with the sort of snobbery he'd dealt with his entire life. Nor was she the same as the other trust fund babies he'd known. There was something irresistible about her. Something that appealed on every possible level. Even more important, she carried his child, which meant that whether she realized it or not, he was going to take control of both her and her pregnancy, starting now.

"I'll be happy to take you home." He waited until the relief gleamed in her violet-blue eyes. "On one condition."

She folded her arms across her chest. "This is not a business negotiation," she snapped.

Oh, but it was. She just didn't realize it, yet. "This is my child, too. As I said, I want to be involved from day one." He offered a crooked smile. "Actually, I was involved on day one.

Now, I want to be involved in the next step. I want to go with you to the doctor."

"Absolutely not."

"Emma, it would be a mistake to shut me out. I'll simply find a way to go around you. It would be far easier to cooperate."

"Once I confirm the pregnancy, we'll get together and discuss how we plan to handle the matter from that point on. But I need time to come to terms with what's happening."

He wasn't about to give her that time. He didn't know her well enough to risk what she might do while he sat around twiddling his thumbs. He didn't answer, though she took his silence for acceptance, assumed she'd gained the upper hand in their little skirmish. Turning on her bare heel, she stalked to the bedroom, returning with her clothes, shoes and BlackBerry.

"Don't bother to show me out." So calm. So cool. So proud. So determined to make An Exit. "I'll call a cab."

He eyed the BlackBerry, then glanced toward the couch where she'd sat the night before and sipped herbal tea. He shrugged. "Okay."

She opened the front door and gently closed it behind her, demonstrating her ability to make An Exit that was also calm, cool and proud. He waited, counted to ten, then crossed to the table beside the couch and picked up Emma's BlackBerry. Next, he headed for the bedroom to collect his car keys. The soft knock sounded at the door seconds before he reached it.

He opened the door and lifted an eyebrow. "Forget something?" Like who was actually in charge around here?

He had to hand it to her, she maintained her poise with impressive fortitude. "I think we mixed up our cell phones."

"We, huh?"

Her chin came up. "Yes. We."

"Come on. I'll drive you home."

"I said—"

"I know what you said, Emma. You want your BlackBerry back?" He didn't wait for her response. He exited the condo, striding past her toward his Ferrari. "Then stop giving me grief and let's go."

Emma Worth had a lot to learn about him, Chase decided. Like the small fact that he didn't like being thwarted. But she'd get the message.

Soon. Very soon.

"Hello, sweetheart. Thanks for letting me know our appointment was *this* Monday morning." He glanced down at his BlackBerry and frowned. "For some reason I didn't have it scheduled."

Emma froze in the doorway between the examination area of the doctor's office and the waiting room and stared in disbelief at Chase. It had been less than forty-eight hours since they parted and yet he sat in one of the chairs, the ankle of one leg resting on the knee of the other in a typically masculine pose. A parenting magazine sat open on his lap. He flipped the magazine closed and tossed it onto the stack of similar periodicals spread across the glass-and-chrome table in front of him.

Her gaze darted to the other occupants in the waiting room and she worked hard—very hard—to keep her voice low and even. "What are you doing here?"

"Waiting for you, of course. The nurse offered to let me join you."

Emma drew in a deep breath. "Did she?" She turned to close the door behind her, using the few precious seconds it offered to regain her equilibrium.

"She did," Chase confirmed. "Next time I'll take her up on her offer."

It was a warning, as clear as though he'd shouted it. Clutching the various pieces of literature the doctor had given her to study, along with an ultrasound photo of their baby, she forced herself to walk briskly across the waiting room toward the exit. Chase stood, pocketed his BlackBerry and followed her. She managed to keep her temper until they reached the parking lot and were standing where they couldn't be overheard.

Then she turned on Chase. "How dare you? How dare you!"

Apparently, he dared plenty because he didn't appear to appreciate the extent of her outrage. If anything, his features settled into a stone-hard cast. "You knew I wanted to be at that first appointment."

"Why?" She jabbed a finger into his chest, allowing her anger free rein. "In order to be with me? Or in order to ask whether you could get an immediate paternity test?"

He planted his fists on his hips and bowed his head for a moment before shooting her a straight look. "I have the right to know whether the baby is mine."

"Oh, for…" She took a deep breath. Getting upset wasn't good for her and it certainly wasn't good for the baby. "I'm done with this conversation."

"Not a chance." He glanced around the downtown district adjacent to the medical building and gestured toward Bistro by the Sea—or the Bistro as the locals referred to the small deli and coffee shop. "Come on. We can grab a couple coffees and talk there."

She didn't bother to resist. They had to have this out at some point. Better someplace where they could conduct their conversation with enough privacy to speak frankly, but in a public setting so she could get up and walk away whenever she'd had enough of Chase's frankness.

He chose an outdoor table in the sun, one well out of the reach of the crisp northern breeze. Excusing himself, he went inside and returned a few minutes later with a large coffee for himself. Instead of another for her, he'd been considerate enough to purchase an herbal tea. Then he took a seat and regarded her thoughtfully.

She decided to take the offensive. "How did you find out about my appointment?" she demanded.

"I made a few phone calls to local obstetricians 'confirming' your appointment until I hit the right doctor's office. I had a feeling you weren't going to include me and surprise, surprise, I was right. That didn't change the fact that I wanted some answers and intended to get them."

"No, you wanted to prove to me that if I don't play this your way, you intend to take control of the situation."

"That, too."

Her mouth compressed. "I gather you're used to getting your own way." Why that should surprise her, she couldn't say. She'd grown up with a father who shared the exact same mindset.

He shrugged. "What I'm used to and what I get aren't always the same thing. These past few days should have shown that much, if nothing else. What I'd appreciate right now are some straight answers."

Emma sighed. "Chase, I don't think I can be any clearer or more straightforward with you. The baby is yours. Despite what you've apparently heard, I don't sleep around."

"Right."

His voice and expression said it all, screamed his disbelief, and she fought back the impulse to lash out. Damn Rafe Cameron and his assumptions. She didn't doubt for a minute he'd influenced Chase with his unfounded assumptions about her. Nor could she totally blame him for believing anything and everything his brother might have said. Since she'd indulged in a one-night stand with Chase, why not with other men?

"Look," she said, hanging on to her patience by a thread. "I'm not sure why this is any of your business, but since there's an outside chance you think it has some bearing on the health of our baby, I'm willing to tell you that I haven't had sex with anyone other than you in two years. That's when I broke up with the man I'd been seeing since my sophomore year in college. Before that, I slept with my high school boyfriend the summer after we graduated from high school. It ended when we both went off to different colleges."

"Fair enough."

"And you?"

He smiled at the pointed question. "I'm thirty-three, so I confess to having a few more relationships than that. The shortest was a one-night stand last November. The longest lasted three years and ended six months ago."

"What happened?" Emma couldn't resist asking.

He shrugged. "She met someone else."

"Someone else? Really?" Emma couldn't say why that surprised her. "Was she upfront about it?"

"Yes, although I've known women who weren't as honest."

He made the admission with amazing calm, totally divorced from sentiment. It gave her pause on two fronts. First, this wasn't the same man who'd taken her to his bed. That man had been the most passionate she'd ever known, a far cry from this cold-blooded, manipulative business tycoon. And second, it worried her that he could so completely cut off his emotions in regard to an issue charged with emotion. Would he do that with her? With their baby?

Time to find out.

"I have no objection to proving paternity after the baby is born," she informed him. "But not before. The doctor warned that in utero tests run the risk of miscarriage and I won't take the chance. Not when it isn't necessary. Not when I'm one hundred percent certain you're the father."

He absorbed the information before nodding his acceptance. "It would be foolish to take any chances with the baby's safety. That doesn't change the fact that I wanted to be there today to ask questions of my own." He shoved his coffee to one side. The booklets she'd collected from the doctor's office snagged his attention, along with the glossy photo the sonologist had handed her following the ultrasound. Something fragile and heartrending shifted across Chase's face. "Is that our baby?"

She slid the photo over the tabletop toward him, moved by the unguarded glimpse she'd caught of his reaction. "The doctor confirmed that I'm approximately nine weeks along."

"Nine weeks?" Alarm combined with suspicion. "But we were together seven weeks ago, not nine."

She nodded in understanding. "Yeah, that threw me at first, too. But the doctor explained that they start counting the pregnancy from the first day of my last period. So, even though conception occurred seven weeks ago, I'm considered nine weeks along."

"Got it." He leaned in and analyzed the gray and white swirls. "That lima bean in the middle…" He cleared his throat. "Is that our baby?"

She offered up a smile, one that felt shaky around the edges. "Yup. That's Junior."

He studied the photo for several long minutes. Taking a deep breath, he switched his attention to her, more determined than she'd ever seen him. "We have to come to some sort of agreement, Emma. An understanding of how we're going to handle your pregnancy from this point forward. You're intent on protecting your privacy and I'm intent on invading it—all because of our baby."

"Our?" She leaned on the word.

"Are you saying there have been other men?" he shot right back.

"Of course not." Emma closed her eyes, fighting for a matching dispassion. "So what now?"

"Now we discuss what happens after the baby is born."

She hesitated. "I agree," she said slowly. "But you have to keep in mind that I just found out I was pregnant on Saturday. This is Monday. I need more than two days to come to terms with everything."

"Can't we come to terms with everything together?"

The question caught her off guard and without a ready answer. Even so, she had the sneaking suspicion that in the few hours between Saturday and Monday he'd already put a game plan in place. Probably in the few minutes they'd been sitting here, he'd been busy fine-tuning it. While she dealt with the emotional issues resulting from her pregnancy, he was busy running every play in the book. Chase was the logical type, someone who thought things through very carefully. She'd be willing to bet his game plan was equally logical and well thought out.

"I don't understand. Why do we have to come to terms with my pregnancy together?" she asked at length.

"Because I'd like to be involved in any decisions you make." He held up a hand when she started to speak. "I don't mean make them for you or argue over your choices. I mean I'd like to have calm, rational conversations during which we discuss all the possible options. Conversations like this one."

"Why?" she repeated, genuinely curious this time.

Something odd moved in his gaze. "I won't have such a serious decision simply handed to me, my fate determined by the whims of another person."

Okay, that felt like old history invading present events. "I gather that's happened to you before?"

"You might say that." His eyes turned a tempestuous shade of blue. "I won't let it happen again. And I won't let it happen to any child of mine."

"You live in Manhattan, don't you?" At his nod of confirmation, she frowned. "How long will you be staying here in Vista del Mar?"

"As long as Rafe needs me to finalize the buyout of Worth Industries."

Emma flinched. "You might not be aware of the fact, but I'm not in favor of the sale." Maybe this wasn't the best time to mention that fact, but she couldn't help herself. She flat-out didn't trust Rafe Cameron. "Why does Rafe want my father's business?"

One minute Chase regarded her in an open, easygoing manner and the next his expression turned blank. "It doesn't matter why Rafe wants it. He has the money to purchase it and your father is willing to sell, despite any objections you may harbor."

Emma shook her head in dismay. "How are we supposed

to work things out?" she asked softly. "We're on the opposite side of every issue."

"We'll negotiate the issues and find a compromise we can both agree on."

She laughed, though the sound contained a hint of tears. "Do you hear yourself? Negotiate? Compromise? This isn't one of your million-dollar business deals we're discussing. It's a child's life."

"Trust me, I'm well aware of what's at stake." He collected their empty cups and disposed of them in a nearby receptacle. Continuing to stand with his back to her, he added, "I've lived through it."

She stiffened. "What are you talking about?"

"I'm talking about the fact that my parents were never married. I'm talking about the fact that I was labeled a bastard from day one. I'm talking about the fact that I'll never allow any child of mine to go through what I did." He swung around, his eyes like slate and his jaw set at an uncompromising angle. "I'm talking about marriage, Emma."

Four

Chase watched every scrap of color drain from Emma's face.

She stared in disbelief. "You cannot be serious."

"I'm dead serious," he assured her.

She moistened her lips and he could see her groping for understanding. "Let me get this straight," she said. "You expect me to marry you because your parents weren't?"

He nodded. "In a nutshell, yes."

"Because people labeled you a bastard?"

He hesitated. As the clock edged closer to midmorning, pedestrian traffic in the area picked up and he didn't want to risk their conversation being overheard. Before he could suggest a change in venue, a cheerful voice rang out.

"Emma! Emma, over here!" A lovely woman in her mid-twenties approached, her dress a vibrant splash of sunset hues that hugged her shapely curves. Dark brown hair curled softly around her face, drawing attention to beautiful espresso eyes that sparkled with pleasure. "Fancy meeting you here," she said, enveloping Emma in a tight hug. "I was hoping I'd run into you before I returned to Los Angeles."

Emma returned the hug with a laugh. "Ana, how great to see you." She pulled back. "Are you just down for the day or all week?"

"Just the day, I'm afraid." She made a face. "Then it's back to the grindstone."

Emma's brows drew together, revealing her concern. "The grindstone? I thought you loved your costume design job, not to mention helping to dress all those fabulous Hollywood stars."

Ana spared Chase a quick glance. "I'll tell you about it later," she murmured, then turned to him and offered a bright smile, along with her hand. "I didn't mean to intrude on your conversation. I'm Ana Rodriguez."

Emma shook her head in dismay. "I'm so sorry. Ana, this is Chase Larson, Rafe Cameron's brother. Rafe is negotiating the purchase of Worth Industries from Dad."

Ana's gaze grew speculative. "I heard there might be a change in ownership, though I never thought I'd live to see the day."

"Nor did I," Emma said with feeling. "Ana and I consider each other sisters," she explained for Chase's benefit. "We were raised together from the time I was ten. Her mother, Nilda, is our housekeeper. And her father was our gardener until he retired. He redesigned the entire landscaping of the grounds and oversaw the installation of our greenhouse. I swear, every last one of Juan's fingers is a green thumb."

Ana glowed with pride. "Absolutely true, every word."

"And you're a costume designer? I don't suppose you also design your own clothing?" Chase asked. He indicated the dress she wore. "This, for example?"

Rosy color bloomed in Ana's cheeks. "As a matter of fact, I did."

"Impressive." There was no doubting the sincerity in his voice. "I'm sure you've heard this before, but you are seriously talented. You could have one hell of a career in New York if you ever decide to go into clothing design rather than costume."

"Well, thanks." She flashed a grin at Emma. "I like this guy. You should hang on to him."

Emma shot Chase a wry look. "I don't think I could get rid of him if I tried."

Ana laughed. "Listen, I have to run. But let's get together the next time I'm in town."

"I'd like that. Call and we'll set something up."

With a final hug, the two women parted. Chase waited patiently until Ana was out of earshot before turning to Emma. "We need to go someplace private where we can talk," he stated. "Clearly, this isn't it."

"We can be as private as you want. It still isn't going to change anything. I'm not going to marry you," Emma warned.

"And I'm not going to discuss the subject standing on a sidewalk in the middle of Vista del Mar." He paused to consider. "Why don't you follow me to the condo?"

She shook her head. "That feels too much like your territory."

So much for that idea. "Well, I flat-out refuse to have this discussion at the Worth estate."

Emma considered their options. "Okay, I know a place. We can take my car." She gestured toward the medical building parking lot, daring to tease, "Unless, of course, you don't consider that territory-neutral enough. I wouldn't want my Beemer to intimidate you."

"It'll be a challenge," he deadpanned. "But I'll do my best not to let your car throw off my negotiating skills."

"What a relief. Tell you what, I'll even drive you back here, afterward. With luck, no one will catch us fraternizing."

"Why does this feel like we're sneaking around?"

Emma smothered a laugh. "Because we're sneaking around?"

"Yeah, that must be it."

Her expression sobered. "Come on. Let's get this over with."

Chase bit back a sharp retort. The ramifications of her pregnancy weren't something to get over, any more than their child was. He forced himself to remain patient and hold fire while they crossed the street to her BMW, a pretty white Cabriolet convertible with tinted windows and a hard-shell top that was currently up instead of retracted behind the backseat.

Emma drove through the downtown area toward the ocean and took the winding coast road that climbed above the city. Redbud, acacia and palm trees, as well as the occasional creosote bush, filled in the dots between gorgeous ocean-view homes. It didn't take long to reach her destination, a secluded bluff high above Vista del Mar with a view of both the town and the ocean.

"Let me guess," Chase said. "The local Lover's Lane?"

"Something like that, though not at this hour," Emma replied. She set the parking brake and swiveled in her seat to face him. "Actually, it's called Busted Bluff."

He choked on a laugh. "Busted Bluff? I'd forgotten that. That's what the locals called this place, isn't it?"

She shared in his amusement. "That's right. When the cops started cracking down on all the kids who'd come up here to drink and party."

"And make out?"

"And make out," she confirmed with a tiny smile.

"How many times did you get busted?"

"Never." She sounded scandalized at the mere idea. "My father would have had my head, the keys to my car and various body parts of any boy reckless enough to be caught messing with me."

"So you never came up here and fooled around?"

She grinned. "I didn't say that, now did I?" Her smile faded, perhaps because she'd "fooled around" last November and now

faced the unexpected consequences. "What do you say we skip
the idle chitchat and get serious?"

"Especially since our situation is serious?"

"Very." She released a sigh rife with frustration. "You just
proposed marriage in order to prevent our child from being
labeled a bastard." She made a sweeping gesture with her hand.
"Why don't you pick it up from there, since I wouldn't begin
to know where to go with it."

"When you put it like that—"

"What other way is there to put it?" Her pansy-blue eyes
filled with a sharp intensity. "I get that you don't want history
repeating itself. But I need more information. Why don't you
start with your parents. Explain to me what happened with
them. You said they weren't married, right?"

"My family dynamics are complicated," he warned. "Here,
let me show you."

He searched through his pockets and pulled out a pen and
notepad. It only took a moment to create a quick chart listing
the key players. He leaned in toward Emma to show her what
he'd written.

A soft, potent fragrance drifted off her. He couldn't tell
whether it was a combination of perfume, soap and shampoo,
or just her natural scent. Whichever, he found it swamped his
senses and kicked in the irrepressible urge to do far more with
her than sit in a car and explain his various family connections.
Other than the light January breeze buffeting the car, the only
sound was the quiet give-and-take of her breath. The knowledge
that he could change it to something faster and more urgent
threatened to overwhelm him.

One kiss and he could alter the entire tenor of the
moment.

She must have picked up on his thoughts because she drew
back. "Not now, Chase."

He shot her a hot, ravenous look. "You sure?"

"Positive." But she didn't look positive. In fact, she looked
just as hungry as he felt.

He reached for her and tugged her toward him. "How positive?"

"This positive."

Her arms came around his neck and she pulled him down so she could take his mouth in a blistering kiss. How was it possible? Back in November she was supposed to have been a one-night stand, and yet the morning after when he'd discovered her gone, he had wanted her every bit as much as the first time he set eyes on her. Then when he'd found her again, he'd tried to sate his need for her—several times, in fact—and it still didn't make a bit of difference to how he felt now.

One touch and he was desperate to have her again. She was pregnant with his child and all he could think was thank God he didn't need a condom, since he sure as hell didn't have one on him.

He tore off his suit coat and tossed it into the back of the car, followed by the purse she'd placed as a barrier between them. He must have missed the seat because he could hear the bounce and spill of the contents. Later. They could reorganize later. Right now, he needed to touch her. Kiss her. Feel her silken flesh under his hands and wrapped around his body.

The buttons of her blouse surrendered beneath his assault, and he next tackled the tiny catch of her bra. Why the hell didn't they make the fastening large enough for a man to unhook it without requiring a magnifying glass and surgical instruments? Finally the scrap of silk and lace parted, allowing him to stroke the fullness of her breasts.

She moaned into his mouth and he pulled back slightly, not certain if the sound was one of pain or pleasure. "Am I hurting you?"

"Not really. My breasts are sensitive, but good sensitive if you know what I mean."

"Not even a little, but if it feels good that's all that matters."

"It feels wonderful."

Chase pulled Emma up and over the small console that

separated the two seats so she sat on his lap, facing him, her legs parted and resting on either side of his. The flowing silk of her skirt rode high on her thighs. Her blouse hung open and her sweet breasts trembled in front of him, just at kissing height. He took immediate advantage.

Her head fell back and another moan sighed from between her lips. He slipped a finger along her velvety inner thigh to the crotch of her panties and dipped inward. She instantly came apart in his hands. He didn't think he'd ever seen anything more glorious.

He started to reach for the zip of his trousers, then hesitated. Instead his hands slipped farther upward beneath her skirt and splayed across her abdomen. He found it almost impossible to believe that his child dwelled there, safe and snug, and not much larger than the lima bean it resembled.

Chase leaned in and pressed his mouth to the section of skirt covering their child. "Hey, bean," he whispered.

The full ramifications hit him then and he closed his eyes and rested his head back against the leather seat. A baby. Dear God, a baby. He looked at Emma. Her mouth and cheeks were ripe with color, and passion glittered in those gorgeous forget-me-not eyes. Even knowing she carried his child, he still wanted to make love to her.

"I can't remember the last time I did this in a car," he murmured.

"I can. Right here on my eighteenth birthday." She winced, the memory causing the desire to leach from her. "Dear heavens, what in the world am I doing?"

"Making love," he offered helpfully. Or maybe it was hopefully.

She pulled back and swept the edges of her blouse closed. "Making love. In a car in the middle of the day on top of Busted Bluff. Pregnant, no less."

"Seems appropriate, don't you think?"

She laughed despite herself. "Not even a little," she informed him with mock severity.

She scrambled off his lap and climbed over the console, back into the driver's seat, somehow still looking graceful and elegant in the process. He couldn't help but notice that her fingers trembled as she rehooked her bra and buttoned her blouse, tucking it into the waistband of her skirt. He also couldn't help but notice the glint of frustrated desire that remained in her eyes.

Before he could act on that desire, she glanced around. "What happened to your notebook and that little chart you drew for me?"

He released a gusty sigh. Time to throttle back. Both of them were far too old to be screwing around in a car. What if someone had driven by and seen them? A town this small, the news would have spread faster than wildfire whipped by a Santa Ana wind. "I tossed it in the back with your purse. Hang on."

He leaned over the seat and shoved through the paraphernalia littering the floor from when he'd upended her purse. It took a minute before he unearthed the notepad. His BlackBerry was resting on top of it where it must have fallen out of his jacket and he grabbed that, as well, shoving it into his pocket. Emma leaned in and tapped the diagram he'd drawn.

"Okay, explain this to me."

He pointed to the circle in the center of the page. "That's my mother, Penny Larson."

"Your mom's a circle?"

"Actually, she's more of a free-form design, but circles and squares and the occasional triangle are the extent of my artistic ability."

"Got it. So, go on, who's the big messy square?"

"My father." His mouth tightened. "While working at Worth Industries, my mom met and had an affair with New York *über*-businessman Tiberius Barron—The Barron, as I tend to call him—who was in town working one of his mega-million-dollar deals with Ronald Worth. I was the result of their affair."

"I've heard of Tiberius Barron. But then, who hasn't, right?" She waved her hand. "Go on."

He pointed to the far side of the page where Hannah and Bob Cameron were listed. "Hannah is Rafe's mother. When she became pregnant with Rafe, your father fired Hannah and Bob for breaking his no-fraternization rule."

Emma paled. "That can't be right," she insisted in a stilted voice. "My father never had such a ridiculous rule. Since practically everyone living in Vista del Mar is employed by Worth Industries, the only way it would work is if everyone in town were celibate."

"I assure you, it was a rule at that time. Or perhaps the rule only applied to Hannah and Bob for some reason. At this point in the game it hardly matters. It's ancient history." Chase tapped his pen against their names. "The two left Worth Industries, married and had Rafe. Unfortunately, Hannah died from COPD—chronic obstructive pulmonary disease— the year Rafe turned fifteen. A few years later my mother, Penny, and Rafe's father, Bob, married. I was in my first year of college, Rafe in his senior year of high school. After Rafe graduated, the Camerons, who by then included my mom, all relocated to Los Angeles. Bob and Mom still live there."

Emma's brows tugged together. "That makes you and Rafe stepbrothers, not real brothers."

Chase's mouth tightened. "When you introduced me to Ana Rodriguez, you said you were as close as sisters. Is she any less your sister because she isn't related to you by blood?"

"Okay, I get your point, but…" She nibbled at her lower lip. "I don't remember you growing up around here, only Rafe."

Chase nodded. "That's because I didn't. When I turned ten I moved to New York to live with my father. I was known as Barron's Bastard from that point on."

"Why did you stay in New York and put up with it?" she asked, appalled. "Why didn't you just move back home with your mother?"

A wintry coldness wrapped around him, filled with dark, painful memories. "Let's just say The Barron made me an offer I couldn't refuse and leave it at that, shall we?"

"But—"

He cut her off. "Which brings us to the issue of the baby. If it's mine, I refuse to have my son or daughter raised a bastard."

"If," Emma repeated. She lifted an eyebrow at his sharp glance. "You still have doubts, don't you? Even though you're the one who's hot to get married in order to spare our baby the humiliation of being called Worth's Bastard, some part of you wonders if I'm really pregnant with your child. I mean, isn't that what this is all about?"

"Yes."

"So let's say we marry…" She stepped behind her Princess Worth facade, making her expression impossible to read. "That means you'll have to trust me when I say that the baby really is yours, because I'm not risking a miscarriage just to give you six-plus months' worth of peace of mind."

He considered, weighed the odds for several long moments, then nodded. "Fair enough. I'm willing to accept the possibility of error and deal with the consequences if you're mistaken. It's more important to ensure the baby bears my name, even if we later establish that he isn't mine."

"You're unbelievable, you know that?"

She jerked the car door open and jumped out, slamming it behind her. Wrapping her arms around her waist, she crossed to stand along the edge of the bluff. Chase joined her, pulling her back a few feet from the crumbling sandstone. The beach below was riddled with rocks and pebbles while white-capped waves crashed toward the shoreline. A short way out intrepid surfers in wetsuits looked like seals lounging on their boards, waiting for the perfect wave.

"Look, Emma, I know neither of us wants marriage. But we have to think of what's best for the child. At least let me give him the protection of my name. If you want a divorce after he's born, fine."

She stiffened within his hold. "You think divorce is better than illegitimacy?"

"In my book, yes."

She spun around to face him. "Well, not in mine. I've seen firsthand what an unhappy marriage can do to the children of that union. They're the ones who ultimately suffer, and I won't put any child of mine through that sort of trauma."

"We're not talking about a real marriage, merely a temporary one."

She lifted her chin in a proud gesture. "I don't need to marry to give my baby legitimacy. The Worth name will protect him or her."

"The Barron name didn't protect me," he shot back. "And it carries far more weight than your name does. Nor will I allow people to make snide comments about the bastard having a bastard. That's just not going to happen."

"And how are you going to stop it?" she demanded. "You can't force me to marry you."

"Everyone has their price, Emma. Even you."

He couldn't have insulted her more if he'd slapped her. Bright color carved a path across her cheekbones. "You're wrong," she retorted in a tight voice.

"Am I?"

He closed the distance between them. He could see her pulse rate kick up, heard the unevenness in her breathing. Beneath her anger and outrage, desire lurked. She might resist, but it was there all the same. He leaned in, watching the conflict build in her eyes. Just as she teetered on the edge of surrender, he pulled back.

"See? It's just a matter of finding the right price."

"I think this conversation has gone on long enough."

She gave him a wide berth on her return to the car. He wasn't the least surprised when she started the engine with a roar, and reversed in a plume of sand and dirt. The tinted driver's side window lowered. "Call someone to come and rescue you. I'm sure you won't have any trouble if you offer the right price." And with that, she drove off.

That went well, Chase congratulated himself. Maybe for

his next career he should consider diplomacy. Clearly, he was a natural. He reached in his trouser pocket for his BlackBerry. It wasn't until he accessed it that he realized that at some point during their embrace in the car, they'd swapped phones again.

Damn it, damn it, damn it!

Emma deliberately slowed her descent from the bluff, giving careful focus to the curves of the road. How could she have allowed herself to fall into Chase's arms again? There wasn't one thing, not one single item, that the two of them shared in common other than their baby.

Well, and their sexual reaction to each other.

No. She refused to consider that something they had in common. Not any longer. She didn't care how gorgeous a body Chase possessed, or the fact that it rippled with lean, ropy muscles. Or how aesthetically appealing his hard, masculine features were. Or how attractive she found the sharp intelligence in those storm cloud-blue eyes. She tightened her grip on the steering wheel. Or how amazing that mouth of his felt against her lips. Against her skin. Against—

Her BlackBerry warbled from the backseat and with an exclamation of annoyance, she pulled over to the side of the road and threw the car in Park. She turned to check the backseat and realized that at some point her purse had been upended and all the various sundries she felt obliged to carry around were scattered across the plush carpeting.

She recovered the phone and took the call. "If this is you, Chase, you can just forget about it. I'm not coming back for you." A long pause followed her outburst and she realized she really should have checked the caller ID before speaking. "Chase?"

"Actually, I'm trying to reach Chase." The deep cool voice rumbled in her ear. "Who is this and why are you answering his phone?"

"This isn't his phone, it's—" She broke off. Oh, no. Please,

please, please don't let it have happened again. They couldn't have mixed up their phones. Not again. She retreated into the sort of unruffled formality that had been drummed into her from birth. "Who is this, please?"

"Rafe Cameron."

It just figured. It truly did. "I don't suppose you called the wrong number?" she asked hopefully.

"Doubtful. I have Chase on both speed and voice dial. Mind telling me who this is?"

She didn't want to tell him. She really didn't. It would raise far too many questions, questions she wasn't prepared to answer at this point in time. "I'll give Chase your message," she said abruptly and disconnected the call.

Then she lowered her head to the leather-padded steering wheel. It took every ounce of self-possession to keep from weeping. Hormones, no doubt. She'd heard about them affecting pregnant women. It would appear she was about to have firsthand experience.

As soon as she recovered her composure, she executed a cautious U-turn and returned to Busted Bluff. Chase stood in the shade beneath a eucalyptus tree, his arms folded across his chest, simply waiting. She pulled up next to him, refusing to so much as glance his way when he opened the door and slid into the seat beside her. She tossed his BlackBerry in his direction.

"Your brother called. I'm afraid you'll have some explaining to do when you get up with him."

Chase winced. "He knows I was with you?"

She fought to control her blush. "I didn't give him my name."

"That'll only make him all the more determined to find out who you are and why you answered my phone." Chase dismissed the problem with a careless shrug, then reached in his pocket and pulled out her BlackBerry. He stuck it in the console between the two seats. "I'll get back to him later."

Silence descended while she took the shoreline road into

town. "I'm sorry I drove off and left you," she said at last. "It was rude."

"That's all right. You're allowed to be rude every now and then. I promise not to allow it to affect my opinion of the Worth name." He spared her a hard glance. "That doesn't change the fact that we're going to have to resolve our differences at some point."

"Not today, Chase, okay? Give me a few days to think things through and discuss the situation with my father."

"I assume he won't be happy."

"To put it mildly."

"Hmm." Chase drummed his fingers on the armrest. "Should I wear a bulletproof vest when I come to see you?"

"That might be wise." She pulled into the parking lot of the medical center where Chase had left his car. She still couldn't bring herself to look at him, not when her hold on her emotions remained so tenuous. "I'll call you."

"I'll be waiting." He captured her chin in his hand and turned her face to his. "Make it soon, Emma."

And then he leaned in and stole a fast, devastating kiss, an uncompromising one that smashed through her defenses and warned that he wouldn't give her any quarter. She wished she could resist him, tried to resist. But something deep inside responded to him, rendering her utterly helpless to his touch. The instant she recognized the sensation, she pulled back.

No. Never. She would never allow a man to make her feel helpless. She'd never be dependent on a man for her happiness. She'd never risk falling in love with him to the extent that her world revolved around his. Nor would she give him control over her mind, body, or spirit.

She'd never make the same mistake her mother made with her father.

"I'll call when I'm darn good and ready to call," she informed him tightly.

He snagged his jacket from the backseat and slung it over

his shoulder. "Make sure 'darn good and ready' happens real damn soon."

Without another word, she put the car in gear and drove away. Not that she got far. Her phone rang again and with a exclamation of irritation, Emma pulled over again. She didn't know why she didn't just let it go to voice mail. Maybe because of that last mix-up with Chase. Or more likely because she suspected it was Chase. Slipping into a convenient parking spot, she snatched her BlackBerry from the cubbyhole in the console between the seats. This time she checked the caller ID. Gillian Mitchell. Oops.

She punched the connect button. "Hi, Gillian."

"Emma, glad I caught you. I just wanted to make sure we were still on for lunch today."

"Absolutely. I haven't forgotten." She'd totally forgotten. "At the club, right? Shall we say at the Tidal Pool in an hour?"

"Perfect. I'll see you there."

That gave her an hour to get her head together. There definitely wasn't enough time to have the sort of conversation necessary to tell her father about her pregnancy. Besides, she had no intention of breaking the news to him at Worth Industries. Filling him in about his impending grandfatherhood would have to wait until tonight.

She caught her lower lip between her teeth, wondering if she dared stretch that time frame by a day or two. She glanced over her shoulder before pulling into traffic. Maybe she'd hold off on the big announcement until this weekend. That would give her time to make some basic decisions so her father couldn't steamroller over her with his opinion on the matter. It would also allow her to figure out how to break the news. A text message was one possibility. So was an email. Or both. From several states away.

Precisely an hour later, Emma entered the Tidal Pool and searched the restaurant for Gillian. She found the lanky brunette seated at one of the tables tucked in a corner, working her way through a cup of coffee. Gillian had only landed in Vista del

Mar six months ago and was already making a name for herself as an ace reporter for the *Seaside Gazette*. Emma had a feeling she knew what prompted this sudden urge for a friendly get-to-know-you luncheon meeting.

The sale of Worth Industries.

Gillian, a woman who hovered in that nebulous range between twenty-five and thirty, lounged back in her chair and studied Emma with intelligent green eyes that went well with her long chestnut-brown hair. "So you're the Worth Princess. You definitely look like one, I have to give you that." She flashed a warm smile to show her greeting was meant in a humorous way. She stuck out her hand. "Gillian Mitchell."

Emma shook hands and smiled in return, taking a seat across from the reporter. "You should see me when I'm wearing my tiara and practicing my Sleeping Beauty pose. You'd really be impressed then."

Gillian chuckled. "Actually, my sources tell me that you spend a lot of your spare time working down at the local women's shelter. Have a soft spot for battered women and children, do you?"

Emma hesitated. It took every ounce of self-possession to keep herself from launching into an impassioned commentary on her charity work. Instead, she limited herself to a simple "Yes."

For an instant a look of concern flashed across Gillian's face. "I hope to God it's not from personal experience," she said gently.

Emma took a moment to gather up the bits and pieces of her self-possession. Too bad Chase had left it in tatters. "Fortunately not."

"That's a relief." Gillian signaled the waitress. "What would you like for lunch?"

"A menu might be a nice start."

Gillian grinned, totally transforming her appearance, deepening the natural warmth and friendliness. "Let me guess.

I suppose you're going to want a drink, too." She released a gusty sigh. "Some people…"

"…are never satisfied." Emma returned Gillian's smile. "You're right. If you want to get to know me better, I won't settle for anything less than a full glass of iced tea. And maybe even a refill."

The next half hour flew by and Emma discovered that she sincerely liked Gillian Mitchell. The reporter was sharp, yet kind. And she totally opened up when discussing her two-year-old son, Ethan, and the challenges facing a single mother. They were challenges Emma took to heart since she'd soon be facing the same ones.

"That's why I'm such a huge proponent of It's Time, the local women's shelter," Emma confessed. "Not only does it give women, especially single mothers, a place to go, but it offers them the opportunity to get back on their feet and provide for their families. It gives them back their dignity."

"Exactly," Gillian agreed.

The waitress came, cleared away their luncheon dishes and topped off their drinks. Emma was suddenly aware that they'd spent the entire lunch discussing issues of interest, which she doubted had anything to do with the reason for Gillian's luncheon invitation. "So, why am I really here? I doubt it's to discuss It's Time, although I think the women's shelter would make a great article for the local paper."

"Yes, it would and I promise it's one I'll write. But, no, that's not why I invited you to lunch." Gillian took a deep breath. "I'd like to ask some questions about the sale of Worth Industries to Rafe Cameron."

"On or off the record?"

Gillian pulled out a notepad and pen. "On."

Emma took a moment to consider. Maybe if this meeting hadn't come on the heels of her discussion at Busted Bluff with Chase, she'd have blown off Gillian. But she had concerns about the sale. The whole town did. And maybe if those concerns

were raised in the *Seaside Gazette,* Rafe and her father would
be forced to address them.

"Okay," Emma said. "Let's start with item one, since it's
the most important in my opinion. The status of our employees
after the sale goes through…"

Five

Two days later, Chase punched a button on his BlackBerry and waited for his brother to answer his phone. "We need to talk," he stated abruptly. "Can you meet me at the condo I'm renting in say—" he checked his watch "—twenty minutes."

"Sure. On my way."

Rafe arrived just after Chase, sweeping through the gates in the plush white Mercedes-Benz G-Class he used to drive to work each day. Chase knew it was all part of the image his brother had cultivated over the years to prove that he wasn't that wild, troublemaking Cameron thug, as the good folks of Vista del Mar had considered Rafe during his formative years. That along with his astounding wealth had come sophistication and refinement, even if it was still edged with a hint of Bad Boy. Of course, the bad boy came out in Rafe's black Porsche Panamera Turbo which had been tagged more than once tearing up the back roads around town. But since Chase had also been on the bad boy side of Officer Garcia's ticket book, there wasn't much he could say.

"So who is she?" Rafe asked the moment they entered the condo. "And don't act like you don't know who I'm talking about. A woman answered your cell the other day. Who was it?"

"Emma Worth."

"Son of a bitch, Larson." Rafe spun around and gave Chase a not-so brotherly shove. "Have you lost your damn mind? You know what she is. And you know what I'm trying to accomplish here. What *we're* trying to accomplish. I don't need any added complications because you can't keep your pistol holstered."

"She's pregnant with my baby." Chase hadn't meant to spill the news quite so abruptly. But he wouldn't allow Rafe to say anything that would cause future friction between them.

Unfortunately, Rafe didn't take the hint. He drew himself up to his full six foot one, a Nordic god at his most intimidating. "And you believe her?"

"Yes." Chase said the word with great care and precision. "I believe her."

"Then you're a fool. She's nothing more than a high-class whore. She'll screw anything that walks. The only difference between her and your average streetwalker is that she doesn't get paid for it."

Chase didn't even remember moving, let alone decking his brother. It was the second time since the two men had met that his lightning speed and agility had gotten past his brother's brawn. One minute Rafe stood confronting him and the next he went flying over the back of the couch and slamming into one of the end tables. A lamp crashed to the floor, narrowly missing his head. Chase vaulted over the couch and planted himself above his brother, his hands balled into fists, ready to take Rafe down again if he so much as breathed wrong.

"Let me make this real clear," Chase bit out. "Clear enough to get through that fog of vengeance you've been living in since your mother died. Emma isn't part of this. She's pregnant with my child and I intend to marry her. You got that?"

Rafe stared up at him, his light blue eyes simmering. "I got it. If I stand up will you knock me down again?"

"Only if you call Emma a whore again. You do that and I'll knock your ass straight through the glass slider and halfway to Hawaii."

Rafe waggled his jaw back and forth experimentally. Relieved it still worked, he said, "Fine, fine. Since you put me down here, help me up." Chase took the hand his brother held up and hauled Rafe to his feet. "You haven't hit me since our parents got engaged."

"Haven't needed to. But as I recall, you ran your mouth about my mother on that particular occasion. Didn't think she was good enough for your precious father."

Rafe rolled some of the tension from his shoulders. "You have a real complex when it comes to women, you know that?"

"You're a fine one to talk. Or do I need to mention your mother, Hannah?"

Temper flared anew in Rafe's expression. "Better not or I won't be the only one going out that plate glass door. And I guarantee if I hit you, you'll end up a hell of a lot farther than Hawaii."

"I gather we understand each other."

Rafe reluctantly nodded. "Yeah, we understand each other." He shot Chase a speculative look. "Is it that serious between you?"

"I'm not sure yet." He crossed to the kitchen and jerked open the refrigerator door. Snagging a couple of long-necks, he tossed one to Rafe, followed by a bottle opener. "We're still circling each other, discussing our options."

"Huh." Rafe popped the cap and took a long swallow. "Maybe we can use this."

"Aw, hell."

Rafe waved the bottle in Chase's direction. "No, no. Hear me out. I think this could work. Worth has more pride than common sense. If you hold off on the marriage proposal, we can use that as a chip in our negotiations."

"Have you lost your damn mind? I mean, seriously."

"Think about it," Rafe urged. "He's already making noises about protecting the local workforce. I can't have him put something like that in the contract. Not if I'm going to gut Worth Industries. We tell him you're willing to legitimize his grandbaby in exchange for excluding that clause from the sale and I'll bet he doesn't even blink. Bye-bye, clause."

Chase tipped back his head and took a long, slow drink, hoping the beer would chill his irritation. From the moment he opened the doors of Larson Investments, he'd always prided himself on the quality of the deals he'd helped put together. Until now. This Worth deal felt vaguely sordid. Okay, definitely sordid. He wiped his mouth with the back of his hand before once again dropping another option onto the table, hoping this time Rafe would listen to reason.

"Or," Chase suggested, "you can realize that Worth Industries is a valuable commodity and instead of the scorch-and-burn vendetta you have going, you can update the company and make it even more profitable than it is now, something Worth is too old-fashioned to pull off. You still take him down a notch by proving you're the better businessman."

Rafe's gaze turned bitterly cold. "Worth fired my parents because they had the unmitigated gall to fall in love. Mom was pregnant with me at the time. Helpless. You know how broke we were over the years, how we could barely scrape enough money together to put food on the table. And when Mom was diagnosed with COPD, there wasn't any insurance to pay for her treatment. Dad went to Worth, begged for his help. And he turned his back on us." Rafe heaved his bottle toward the trash. It hit its mark with a crash. "He let my mother die by inches when all along he knew that damned factory was responsible for her illness."

Chase had heard the story. Had heard Rafe describe those months in hideous detail. "Tearing apart the factory won't bring her back. But it will hurt a lot more people than just Ronald Worth."

Rafe's jaw assumed a stubborn slant. "I don't care. They all turned their backs on us. It's time they know how it feels." He regarded his brother for a long moment, frustration eating at him. "Okay, Chase. I'll give you Emma. Protect her from what's about to happen if you can. But Worth is going down. And so is the rest of Vista del Mar, even if I have to pull it apart with my bare hands."

"For God's sake—"

"Enough," Rafe interrupted him. "Listen to me, Chase, because I'm dead serious here. I've been hearing rumors about your pregnant heiress. She's not happy about this sale and she doesn't hesitate to say so. I won't have her causing any trouble. Either you rein her in or I will."

"Rein her in?" Chase snorted. "You have met Emma, right?"

A brief smile touched Rafe's mouth before vanishing again. "I suggest you find a way to control your woman. And soon."

The front door closed behind Rafe. Chase set his empty bottle on the counter with exquisite care. Hell. He'd spent most of his life learning how to dance through minefields. But this... What a mess.

Exhaustion settled over him like a blanket and he scrubbed his face while he considered his options. He could practically hear the clock ticking, narrowing those options with each passing minute. In fact, he could come up with exactly one that would protect Emma, and that was with his name. Somehow, he needed to convince his pregnant heiress, as Rafe had described her, to marry him. It was his best shot at removing her from the playing field. To keep her from becoming a pawn in this hideous game. And there was only one way to convince her to marry him.

The time had come to seduce Emma into compliance.

After the way they'd last parted two days ago, Emma couldn't believe that Chase managed to persuade her to join him for dinner with such ease. But he had. Sometime between the start of the phone conversation and the end, he'd convinced her that they should talk again and that the perfect venue for that conversation was Jacques', one of the most exclusive restaurants in Vista del Mar.

The instant she heard Chase pull up, she grabbed her wrap and headed downstairs. Even so, by the time she reached the foyer, he'd already been escorted into her father's study, where the two men spoke in low voices. It didn't occur to her until just then that she hadn't warned Chase not to mention her pregnancy. If he unwittingly dropped that particular bombshell...

She darted toward the study and flung open the door without knocking. The two men glanced up from a set of blueprints they were examining and eyed her with identical expressions of surprise.

"Oh, there you are," she offered lamely.

Chase studied her through narrowed eyes, noting the rapid give and take of her breath. "You didn't have to run. Henri will hold the table."

"But we wouldn't want to annoy Chef Moreau," she replied. Okay, so judging by her father's expression, the comment sounded totally inane. She smiled brightly at the two men. "Shall we go?"

Ronald gave Chase a proud nudge. "She takes after me. Always on time, that girl. Not one to make you wait around while she changes her dress for the twentieth time or fusses because she didn't get her face drawn on quite straight."

"Good to know." Chase and her father shook hands.

To Emma's profound relief, the men didn't waste any further time on idle chitchat. She and Chase exited the room, crossed the three-story foyer of the Spanish-style stucco mansion and exited out the front door to where Chase had parked his car.

The instant they were enclosed in the privacy of his Ferrari, he shot her a grim look. "You haven't told him yet, have you?"

Emma fastened her seat belt, all the while striving for a calm and casual tone. Instead, she managed to hit somewhere in the vicinity of nervous as hell. "No. And I appreciate your not dropping it on him by mistake during your discussion earlier."

"He's going to have to know, and soon."

Emma closed her eyes. "I'm well aware of that fact, Chase. Please trust me to find the right time."

"I'm not pushing." He started the car with a muffled roar. "Okay, I am pushing. I'm just concerned that word will get out. This is a small town. People gossip."

"But I haven't mentioned it. Other than to you, that is." She swiveled in her seat, allowing a hint of suspicion to show. "Have you told anyone I'm pregnant?"

"You're forgetting Dr. Hastings," he said, which didn't exactly answer her question.

She waved that aside. "Not a chance. He's my doctor. He's bound by rules of confidentiality."

"And are the nurses on his staff bound by those same rules? What about the person who performed the ultrasound? Or the office workers? You don't think that they occasionally talk, especially when it's someone as high profile as the Worth Princess?"

She stiffened. She'd been tagged with that name all her life and had learned to turn it aside with a joke the way she had with the Seaside Gazette reporter, Gillian Mitchell, or to ignore it with icy politeness. But with Chase… For some reason it cut deeper to hear him refer to her that way. "Please don't call me that. Not you, Chase."

He spared her a swift, penetrating glance. "Normally I wouldn't, sweetheart. I don't even think of you that way. I was just making a point." He reached over and brushed her cheek with the knuckles of his hand, a simple stroke of understanding. "I know you well enough to see how far from the truth it is. In fact, I'm one of the few people who gets it. Who's lived beneath the shadow of an uncomfortable label, just like you."

Her hands tightened in her lap. Twisted. "I've never understood why they can't look at me and see the truth. Even your brother has me pegged as a shallow party girl."

"Others don't know you as well as I do." His voice softened, filled with compassion. "They see the outer gloss and think the gloss goes all the way to the bone. They look at me and see a bastard and they don't bother to look any further, either. It's what I am, therefore it must be who I am. You tell me whether being called a princess is better or worse than being called a bastard."

Emma released a sigh. "I haven't lived through what you have, so you know I can't." But their child would if she didn't marry Chase, which was undoubtedly his point.

"Exactly. Any more than I can fully understand your life unless you choose to open the door and let me in."

He stopped at a red light and rested his forearms on the steering wheel. His dark suit blended into the darkness while the slashing line created by his crisp, snow-white cuffs drew attention to his hands. They were powerful hands, capable and long-fingered, gripping the wheel with casual strength. And yet, she'd seen them demonstrate unbelievable gentleness when they'd tripped across her body.

He turned his head to look at her. "You're a Worth, Emma. Add to that the fact that you're pregnant and unmarried. When you put all of those pieces together it creates serious fodder for gossip." He allowed that to sink in before adding, "You don't want your father hearing about this from anyone other than you."

He was right and she knew it. "Fine," she said with a sigh. "I'll tell him in the morning."

"Fair enough." The light turned green and he drifted forward, the streetlights reflecting off the hard angles of his face. "Do you want me there when you give him the good news?"

She was tempted. Sorely tempted. But she couldn't predict how her father would react. At a guess, not well. And she didn't want to risk Chase bearing the brunt of her father's fury.

"Thank you, no, though I'm sure he'll want to talk to you soon enough."

"I don't doubt it." Chase sounded unusually grim. "If we have a daughter I would want to rip apart any man who impregnated her without benefit of a wedding ring."

Emma didn't know what to say to that. Part of her softened at the protectiveness he portrayed toward their unborn child. Another part worried that he'd prove too controlling a parent. Her father had been like that, when he'd bothered to pull his head out of work long enough to pay attention.

Chase spared her another glance. "What is it?"

Emma shrugged off the question. "Nothing important. Just thinking about my father."

"You don't look happy."

"Old history," she replied briefly. "Not worth mentioning."

"Hmm. I think I can guess. I was raised by a father obsessed with business, too, remember?"

It struck her then that she and Chase shared far more similarities than differences. They pulled beneath the stone portico that covered the entrance to Jacques'. A valet leaped forward to open Emma's door and help her from the car. Then he took the key from Chase and, with an expression of keen anticipation, hopped into the Fiorano.

"Thank God I bought full coverage when I rented the thing," Chase muttered.

"He did look a bit too eager, didn't he?" she replied, amused.

The instant they stepped through the heavy wooden doors of the restaurant, the maître d', Henri, greeted them with a broad smile. "Welcome to Jacques', Mr. Larson. Ms. Worth. Your private room is ready for you."

Emma lifted an eyebrow. "Private room?"

Chase inclined his head. "Nothing but the best for our first date."

"First date?" The absurdity of it hit her and she smothered a laugh.

He noticed her amusement and grinned. "Bizarre, isn't it?"

"Very."

How odd to realize that this was, indeed, their first date. Granted, they'd spent one day and night together back in November. But it hadn't been a date, per se, more like two people on a delicious collision course, before they each went their separate ways once again. And since Chase's arrival in Vista del Mar, it had been more of the same. They'd run into each other at the cocktail party celebrating the proposed sale of Worth Industries. Okay, fine, they'd slept together that night. But that hardly qualified as a date. In fact, she'd rather not consider what it did qualify as. Then they'd shared a drink at Bistro by the Sea, followed by a close encounter of the most delicious kind at Busted Bluff. None of those occasions could be considered a true date.

And yet, here she was ten full weeks pregnant with Chase's baby.

Henri escorted them through the elegant dining room with its plush pearl-gray carpeting, soaring ceilings and glass walls overlooking the Pacific. Crystal sparkled and silver gleamed against the linen-covered tables.

At the far end of the restaurant a pair of glass doors, etched with a lovely scene of a tidal pool teeming with sea life, assured full privacy by enclosing them in an intimate room set for two. Two of the walls were glass, one offering a slice of the town, the other a full panoramic view of the ocean. The table was small and intimate with candles throwing off subtle light and ruby-red rose petals scattered across the ivory tablecloth. In the middle of the table several matching roses and a glorious white lily in full bloom floated in a shallow bowl of water.

Henri held Emma's chair, opened the linen napkin folded into the shape of an oyster and placed it neatly in her lap. Then he handed them each their menus. He described the specials for the evening at great length and seemed somewhat taken aback when Chase declined the need for a sommelier.

"You can have something to drink, if you want," Emma said once they were alone.

"I'll order sparkling water." He glanced around the room. Along one wall a fire crackled in a stone hearth. "I understand they open this room during warmer weather."

"Yes, they remove the glass windows and you can either have it open-air or screened. Jacques' will even arrange for a private table on the beach for special occasions."

"I was given that option but it's too chilly tonight. Plus the wind is blowing straight off the water and I'd rather not spend the night picking sand out of my sea bass."

Emma chuckled. "This is a lovely alternative, thank you. The fire is a particularly nice touch."

"I'm glad you like it." He gathered up her hand and interlaced their fingers. "You look stunning, by the way. I can't decide if that dress is red or orange."

"Burnt orange, and thank you." It was one of her favorites, a strapless confection that hugged her breasts and drifted to her ankles in layers of feather-light chiffon. "I was afraid I might be too chilly, but the fire makes it just warm enough."

Emma stared down at their joined hands and then lifted her gaze to study Chase with intense curiosity. Gently, she pulled her hand free of his. "If you don't mind my asking, what are you hoping to achieve by bringing me here?"

"Achieve?"

"You're a businessman, Chase. That means you have a plan." She tilted her head, half amused, half exasperated. "Men like you always have a plan."

He sat back in his chair, so that shadows leaped across his face. They carved deep into the hollows beneath his sky-high cheekbones and turned his eyes to ebony. "Maybe you should clarify what you mean by that."

"When I say men like you?" At his nod, she continued, "Men like you and Dad and Rafe. You all look at the world like it's some giant oyster and you're all trying to figure out the best way to pry it open and seize the pearl inside for your own. Some men just whack at it, willy-nilly. Others sit around and wait, hoping the oyster will open up on its own. Businessmen—"

"—like me, your father and Rafe," he clarified.

"Exactly. Businessmen always have a plan of attack." She took a sip of water and gazed at him over the rim. "Care to share yours?"

"No problem." He snapped open his leather-bound menu and perused the contents. "I plan to seduce you into compliance."

"Really?"

"Really." He peered over the top of the menu and lifted an eyebrow. "How's it working so far?"

She considered. "Fairly well," she admitted. "But it's early yet."

"In that case, I'll wait until after the appetizers."

The appetizers nearly worked. The crab-stuffed artichoke hearts were incredible and if she'd been foolish enough to combine them with wine, she might have crawled right into his lap and let him have his wicked way with her. Again. But the reason she refused the wine—her pregnancy—helped keep her libido in check. Or it did for the most part.

A three-course dinner followed the appetizers, the seafood perfectly cooked and plated. They shared each other's meals, which only deepened the level of intimacy. All the while, Emma waited for Chase to make his first move, curious to see if it would come as a romantic overture or under the guise of "getting to know you better." He chose the latter, much to her distress.

"So, I gather you're an only child, which probably explains the princess label everyone in town is intent on hanging around your neck."

She helped herself to a final bite of sea bass—*sans* blowing beach sand—and steeled herself against the line of questioning he intended to pursue. Very few people knew her entire history. Now that she thought about it, Ana Rodriguez and her parents were probably the only ones aware of the true story, even though they hadn't lived on the estate at the time the events in

question went down. Over the years, she'd chosen to share the
information with them.

The instant Emma locked her emotions under tight control,
she gave Chase the cool, gracious, Princess Worth smile. "You
gather wrong. I have a brother who's five years older. And I even
have three Worth cousins," she added, hoping the information
would distract him. "Becca and her two brothers live in Napa
Valley."

"And your brother?" Chase boomeranged right back where
she didn't want him to go. "I don't recall meeting him."

"That's because you haven't. He...isn't in the picture."

Chase absorbed that for an instant, no doubt surprised his
research hadn't turned up any information on the subject. "He
doesn't work for your father." It wasn't a question.

"You're right. He doesn't."

"Why not?"

"You cut straight to the quick, don't you?" she ventured.
"Just stick your foot right in where it doesn't belong."

"Foot. Nose. Hand." His congenial smile held a ruthless
edge. "Whatever it takes to figure things out."

"Then, why don't I give you the short version?" Emma
pushed her dinner plate to one side and sat very straight and
very still. "My brother went to boarding school at fifteen, which
is also how many years it's been since I last saw him."

Chase's brows drew together in a quick frown. "Hell, Emma,
I'm so sorry." Genuine concern underscored the words. "What
happened?"

She should resent him asking, but it was a reasonable
question, compassionately delivered, and one many in Vista
del Mar would give anything to have answered. "Shortly after
my mother died—" She broke off, horrified to discover she
couldn't continue.

Chase escaped his seat and crouched beside her chair.
"Damn it, Emma, don't. Please don't cry. You don't have to
say anything more if it's going to upset you."

She fought to hold back her tears, wishing she could blame

her emotional reaction on hormones. But it was more than that. "It's painful and not something I talk about. Ever."

"It's your choice, sweetheart." He placed a hand on her bared shoulder and squeezed gently. "I won't think any less of you if you don't want to tell me."

She shuddered beneath his tender touch, but didn't dare surrender to the desire that single caress aroused. It would be all too easy to turn to him. Tumble into mindless passion. But it would lead her down a path overflowing with pitfalls and unpredictable consequences. She forced herself to focus on a bead of condensation gathering along the side of her water glass, hoping the distraction would restore her self-control.

It didn't work. Past events swirled around her like a chill wind. As much as she hated the idea of discussing family history—old, painful, horrible history—maybe the time had come to excise the wound. Chase was here and willing to listen. If they had any hope of creating a future together, one of them needed to take a chance. To let down their guard and trust.

"My mother and brother were close. Very close," she found herself admitting. "When she died, my brother blamed my father."

"Why would he do that?"

Emma shoved back her chair and escaped across the room to stand in front of the fire. For some reason she'd turned icy cold. She held her hands to the blaze. To her horror, she saw they trembled and swiftly dropped them to her sides, praying that Chase hadn't noticed.

Unfortunately, he proved far too observant. He joined her by the hearth and wrapped his arms around her waist, pulling her against the solid strength of his chest. Warmth surrounded her and she leaned into him. "I'm sorry. I can imagine how difficult this must be for you."

She turned in his hold and buried her face against his shoulder. How often had she longed to have someone to hold on to, someone able to see beneath the surface glitter to the woman beneath? A woman with needs and desires, who craved a deep passionate love all her own? Her body curved into his, softened against him, recognized him as an integral part of herself even though every bit of intellect screamed against it.

"You're Rafe's brother," she told him in a muffled voice. "I'm not sure I want to discuss this with you."

He pulled back, the iciness in her veins invading his expression. "You think I'd tell him?"

She hated throwing a barrier between them, but she had no choice but to address the possibility. "I can't be certain," she confessed with unflinching frankness. "If it helped Rafe gain an edge with the sale..." She trailed off with a miserable shrug.

"Let's get something straight." She caught the uncompromising intensity in Chase's voice, an implacability that spoke of honor and pride. "I swear to you that I will not share anything you say to me about private family matters with Rafe."

She searched his face, searching for any sign of deception and saw none. This would be a huge test for her, proof positive of whether she could trust Chase or not. He was her baby's father, which meant that they'd have a lengthy relationship, regardless of the form that relationship took. Tonight could be the start of something amazing, or the beginning of the most difficult road she'd traveled since her mother's death. What troubled her most was how intensely attractive she found Chase, more attractive than any other man she'd ever known. It wouldn't take much to push her past mere attraction into something far deeper and permanent. Into love.

Emma shied from the knowledge, but now that she'd opened the door to that likelihood she found it almost impossible to close again. "Okay, I trust you," she found herself saying. And yet, it was the truth.

"Why did your brother blame Ronald for your mother's death?" he repeated.

He continued to hold her and she realized that he would pick up on every nuance communicated by her body, even inadvertent ones. Especially inadvertent ones. "My mother died of a drug overdose."

Chase stilled in shock. "My God."

"She…" Emma fought the flashes of memory that she'd spent so many years attempting to suppress. "She and Dad had just had a huge fight. Mom accused him of cheating on her."

"Was he?"

She shrugged. "I was nine. What do I know? But since my mother used the word *again*, I'm forced to assume it happened more than once over the course of their marriage. Needless to say, it wasn't a pretty scene."

"You overheard them?"

"My brother and I both did. Dad left the house after the fight. He had a business dinner to attend, or so he claimed. That's when Mom took the sleeping pills. We don't know if it was accidental or deliberate. We'll never know. But my brother found her. He's the one who called 911, who went to the hospital with her."

"Who stayed with you?"

"The housekeeper."

"Ana's mother?" He hesitated, clearly searching for a name. "Nilda?"

"No, they didn't start working for us until after my brother was sent off to boarding school." Emma's brows pulled together. "Funny. I can't remember our housekeeper's name at the time. She left the day after Mom died. We had quite a few others before Dad finally hired Nilda and Juan."

"That's when you latched onto their daughter, Ana?"

Emma blinked, pulled from her reverie. "I didn't *latch* onto Ana. We became friends. Sisters."

An undeniable tenderness infused the manner in which he stroked the curve of her cheek. "Someone to fill the gap left by your mother and brother."

She'd never quite looked at it that way. "I suppose," she conceded.

"I gather you didn't blame your father the way your brother did." He hesitated. "But then, how could you?"

She shook her head in confusion. "Sorry?"

"You didn't have anyone left. If you took a stand against your father, you might get sent away, too. So you became Daddy's Princess."

She drew back. So much for trusting him. He didn't understand at all. But then, how could he? He was a businessman through and through. Whatever buttons he needed to push to achieve his ends, he'd push. "That's one way of looking at it," she stated with cool carelessness. "It's not how I remember it."

"Fair enough."

"I just want you to understand why I won't marry you."

"And why is that?" He asked the question with a matching coolness.

"As I've mentioned before. I saw firsthand what happens when a marriage goes disastrously wrong. It killed my mother. It caused a breach between my father and brother that's never healed. And it left me with all the material wealth a woman could want, without it meeting any of my emotional needs. That's not what will happen with my child."

"History doesn't have to repeat itself."

"You're absolutely right. And I fully intend to see that it doesn't." She crossed to the table and picked up her purse and wrap. She turned to face him with the same implacability he'd shown her on any number of occasions. "That's why I'll never marry you, Chase. I refuse to allow history to repeat itself."

"We're not the same people as your parents," he pointed out. She could hear the hint of controlled anger sweeping through his words.

"You're right. That still doesn't change my answer." She crossed to the etched glass doors protecting their privacy. "Thanks for dinner. It was delicious. But if you don't mind, I'd like to go home now."

Six

Emma didn't have longer than a single night to decide on the gentlest way to inform her father of her pregnancy. All hell broke loose the next morning, although it had nothing to do with the baby she carried and everything to do with the fact that Gillian Mitchell's article appeared in the morning addition of the *Seaside Gazette*.

Ronald Worth reacted first. "Emma!" he roared. "Damn it, Emma, what the hell have you done?"

She appeared in the doorway of the breakfast room just in time to see her father drop his fine-boned Wedgwood cup onto its equally fine-boned Wedgwood porcelain saucer, shattering both. Coffee stained the pristine white tablecloth in a rapidly expanding circle of muddy brown. Nilda would not be pleased.

"You bellowed?" Emma asked lightly.

He shook the paper at her. "What. The. Hell. Is. This?"

"It looks like a newspaper."

His face turned bright red. "Don't get smart with me. I'm

referring to this ridiculous article some upstart reporter by the name of Gillian Mitchell wrote. She's attributing you as one of her sources."

Emma paused by her father's chair long enough to plant a kiss on his overheated forehead. Then she reached for the small bell resting by his right hand and rang it. Their maid, Tia, appeared almost instantaneously, took one look at the coffee disaster and disappeared.

"I haven't read the article, yet," Emma admitted, "so I'm not in a position to comment on it. But I did talk to Gillian a few days ago and discussed some of my concerns regarding Rafe Cameron's purchase of Worth Industries."

"That is none of your business," Ronald informed her in a hard, cold voice. It was the one she called his Industrial Strength Voice, usually reserved for someone about to be fired at Worth Industries. He only directed it toward a family member on very rare occasions. His index finger thudded repeatedly against the coffee-stained table to emphasize his words. "That sale is between me, Rafe and a slew of overpaid financial advisors and shark lawyers. You just stick to your charity work."

His words impacted like a blow. It took every ounce of self-possession to take a seat and face her father without a speck of the hurt she felt showing on her face. "That sale involves all the citizens of Vista del Mar since what Rafe chooses to do with the business will have a dramatic impact on the economy of the town," she corrected smoothly. "I have every right to express my opinions and will continue to do so, whether you, Rafe, your overpaid financial advisors or your shark lawyers like it, or not." She fixed him with a gaze every bit as hard and steely as his own. "And I don't appreciate your dismissing my charity work in that condescending tone of voice."

"It's not a real job," he immediately objected.

They'd had this argument more than once and she'd learned never to give an inch or back away from the confrontation the way her mother had. That path led to disaster. "What you mean is that it's not a paid job. But it is every bit as real as your work at Worth. I help people who are in desperate straits to get back on their feet so that you can hire them to put food on their table without governmental assistance. I volunteer my time because I'm in the fortunate position of not needing the money."

"You could be running Worth. In fact, you should be running the company."

She caught the undisguised frustration and her anger faded, replaced by an aching tenderness. "Oh, Dad." She sighed. "I know how much it hurts that none of your children are interested in stepping into your shoes."

"One of you might be," he muttered.

She couldn't believe he still held out such a forlorn hope. "I'm sorry, Dad. It isn't going to happen. We have to live our own lives, our own way. Sell Worth if that's what you want. Give it away for all I care. But please. I'm begging you. Protect your workers."

Tia reappeared with fresh linens and switched the tablecloth with brisk efficiency. Before she left, she replaced Ronald's cup and saucer, and topped it off with fresh coffee. She also placed a pot of tea on the table for Emma, along with her typical breakfast of fresh fruit, granola and yogurt.

"Thanks, Tia," Emma murmured. Fortunately, her morning sickness had subsided enough for her to look at her breakfast without making a mad dash for the nearest bathroom. "Tell Nilda that Dad apologizes about the coffee, will you?" She gave her father a pointed look.

"Yes, yes, tell Nilda whatever," Ronald said testily. He waved the maid from the room. The instant she disappeared, he slapped the newspaper against the pristine tablecloth. The sound of the impact cracked like a bullwhip. "Now, getting back to this interview—"

"I don't want to talk about the interview until after I've read it. There's something else we need to discuss." She hesitated. "It's serious, Dad."

Emma had to hand it to him. Sometimes he came through, switching from businessman to father in the blink of an eye.

He instantly shoved the paper aside, his brow wrinkling in concern.

"Are you all right?" he demanded. "Did Larson try something last night? Did he hurt you?"

"Yes, I'm all right. Of course Chase didn't try anything last night or hurt me." She fiddled with her fork. No matter how hard she struggled to come up with the perfect words to relay the news, they simply did not exist. "Dad, Chase and I have met before," she began.

Ronald paused in the act of reaching for his coffee cup. "You never mentioned that."

Emma shrugged. "There wasn't any reason to mention it until recently."

He fortified himself with a sip of coffee, his gaze intent through the steam. "What happened recently?"

She took a deep breath. Time to stop circling the announcement like some sort of wary vulture. She'd just say the words and get everything out in the open where they could deal with it. "I'm pregnant, Dad."

His cup tumbled from his hand again and shattered against the saucer. "You're what?"

Once again, coffee stained the pristine white tablecloth in a rapidly expanding circle of muddy brown. Emma sighed. Nilda would definitely not be pleased this time. "Obviously it wasn't planned. But it happened and Chase and I are discussing how we want to handle the situation."

"I'll tell you how you're going to handle the situation." Her father's voice rose to a bellow. "You're both getting married as soon as it can be arranged."

"Dad, your heart. Please calm down."

He battled his temper, fought for his legendary control and then snatched up his medication and tossed back a pill. Since he'd smashed his cup of coffee, he reached for her tea, gulping down a mouthful. "Good lord, how can you stand to drink this stuff?" he demanded the instant he swallowed his pill. Then he waved that aside. "Never mind, never mind. We have far more important matters to deal with, starting with how this happened. Explain it to me, Emma. How the hell did you end up pregnant?"

"In the usual way." Ruddy color began to invade her father's face again and she elaborated, attempting to keep her tone low and soothing. "Chase and I met in New York shortly before Thanksgiving. There was an instant attraction. One thing led to another. Unfortunately, birth control isn't always one hundred percent reliable. Quite obviously it wasn't in our case. I realized a short time ago that I was pregnant."

His color eased slightly, though not nearly enough. "Does Larson know?"

"Yes. As I told you, we're discussing our options."

Before Ronald could reply, someone pounded on the front door. Tia, who must have been lurking in the hallway nearby, opened the door. Chase's voice reverberated across the foyer. "Where is she?"

"Where is who, señor?" Tia asked timidly.

"Emma Worth." His shoes rang across the slate entryway. "Emma? Where the hell are you? We're going to have this out once and for all."

"Speak of the devil," she murmured and pushed back her chair.

"Is that him?" Ronald shot to his feet. "I'll kill him."

She moved to bar his path, planting her hands squarely on his chest. "You'll do no such thing. The three of us are going to discuss this like civilized adults." Though considering all the listening ears, the breakfast room might not be the best venue for that discussion. "Why don't we use your study, Dad?"

They joined Chase in the foyer and Emma deliberately stepped between the two men. "Your timing is impeccable as always, Chase," she informed him. "I was just telling Dad the latest news."

His gaze arrowed from her face to her father's. A distinct wariness swept across his expression. "I gather it didn't go well."

"Good guess." She gestured toward the opposite end of the foyer. "We were about to discuss the situation in the study. I'll have Tia bring more coffee." She glanced over her shoulder at the hovering maid. "Please don't use the Wedgwood this time."

A hint of laughter sparkled in Tia's dark eyes. "No, Ms. Emma."

Chase paced the darkly masculine confines of Ronald Worth's study like a caged cougar. This day had not begun well and didn't promise to improve anytime soon. Rafe's furious call started off his morning, his single demand ringing in Chase's ears. "Fix this!"

By the time he got his hands on a copy of the *Seaside Gazette* and read Gillian Mitchell's inflammatory article, his mood had gone from bad to downright filthy. He intended to have a pointed conversation with Emma. He hadn't planned on having one with her father, too.

The instant Emma closed the door to the study, Ronald swung around, his fists clenched in a manner that suggested it would take damn little provocation for him to use them. He glared first at Chase, then at his daughter. "You'll marry the bastard, by God. You hear me, Emma? I won't have the Worth name dragged through the mud because you two were careless."

Chase took a single step forward, but it was enough to put Ronald on his guard. "Do not call me a bastard," he said in a voice that was very soft and very, very deadly.

"It's what you are, isn't it? Barron's Bastard?" Something in Chase's expression had him raising his hands in clear surrender. "All right. I get the message. I wouldn't want to be known by that name, either. Which is why I won't have any grandchild of mine dealing with that sort of stigma."

"I agree."

Ronald opened his mouth, then shut it again. "Wait a minute. You agree?"

Chase crossed the room to stand with his back to the window. It was an old trick, but one that worked well, concealing his expression while making it difficult for everyone else to conceal theirs. "I'm not the one throwing up roadblocks. Your daughter is."

Ronald swung around. "Emma?"

Her chin jutted out at a familiar angle. How many times had he seen her father assume that exact same pugnacious stance? "I don't agree that marriage is the only option here. Just because Chase was called by that awful name doesn't mean it will happen to my son or daughter."

"Our," Chase reminded her.

Ronald thrust his hands through his hair, standing the neatly trimmed gray strands on end. "Have you lost your mind? What are we supposed to do? Wait and see if it happens?" he objected. "It'll be a little late to do anything about it at that point. The damage will be done."

Chase refused to prolong the argument, especially not with Emma's father wading into the middle, contributing his two cents. Worth was on his side when it came to this subject, which would help in the long run. But that didn't mean he'd use father against daughter. It felt too much like ganging up. "We're not going to wait. We'll marry as soon as I can convince Emma it's the best option."

"Good, good." Worth nodded his approval. "Here's what I suggest the two of you—"

"Nor are we going to discuss it with you," Chase interjected smoothly.

"Now wait a damn minute," Worth began.

Chase didn't give the older man the opportunity to rev into full throttle. His own father responded to opposition the same way. Don't negotiate. Don't argue. Just steamroller right over the problem. Once he took off, it became next to impossible to derail him.

"Ronald, let me assure you that Emma and I will figure out what's best for the two of us and the baby. We'll inform you of any and all decisions the minute we make them." He paused just long enough to allow that to sink in. "That isn't why I came here today."

"That might not be why you're here, but it's what we're damn well going to talk about." Ronald moved to confront his daughter, astonished when Chase stepped forward to block his path. Taken aback by the unexpected maneuver, he hesitated, struggling to regroup. "If Emma's pregnant, you're going to marry her and that's all there is to it," he insisted.

Chase shook his head. "No, it's not. All decisions regarding this baby will be made between two people. And you're not one of them. Nor do I intend to prolong this conversation any further. Not with you." He switched his attention to Emma. She stood with her arms folded across her chest, her stance defensive. "I'm actually here about the article in the *Seaside Gazette*."

Relieved to have something else to dig his teeth into, Ronald slapped his own copy of the newspaper against his open hand. "That's right. I'd almost forgotten. Why would you allow that woman to interview you, Emma, especially without talking it over with me first?"

She lifted an eyebrow. "I can see what's most important to the two of you."

"Not most important," Chase denied, pacing closer. "Just the only issue I intend to address with your father standing in the room. Why in the world would you make such inflammatory remarks? What were you thinking?"

"What was I thinking?" She drew herself up, her flashing eyes reflecting the intensity of her voice. "I was thinking that I don't trust Rafe Cameron as far as I can pick him up and toss him. I was thinking about the employees of Worth Industries and what will happen to them after Rafe gets his hands on the business. I was thinking that I haven't heard one word from any of you fine, upstanding businessmen about the people who will be the most affected by your decisions. That's the employees, in case you've forgotten." She planted her hands on her hips. "So tell me. How do you plan to deal with those concerns?"

"I've already explained that's none of your business," Worth began.

She rounded on her father. "Of course it's my business. It's everyone's business. Our employees are worried about their jobs and what stipulations are in place to protect them." She turned to include Chase in her denunciation. "Rafe Cameron could eviscerate Worth and sell off the pieces bit by bit. Or he could outsource the labor to Mexico. How do we know that he intends to stay and make the changes and improvements that Worth needs to grow and become viable in today's market?"

Chase buried all thought and emotion behind an impregnable mask. Every last one of her points held more validity than she could possibly imagine. Even if he didn't flat-out lie, he knew Rafe's ultimate plans for the business—to strip it down to its bare bones and leave the carcass to rot. Eventually, so would the entire town. Once they did, any hope he had for a relationship with Emma would go straight into the crapper.

Possessing the true facts of the situation also left Chase without a solid defense to offer. He could invent any number of plausible scenarios, but he refused to do that regardless of what Rafe would want, because they weren't true. Right now the expression "between a rock and a hard place" took on a whole new, gut-wrenching meaning.

"What would it take to convince you that Rafe's on the up-and-up?" Ronald asked, the question edged with a touch of desperation.

"Written guarantees would be nice."

Chase nearly groaned. He needed to stop the direction of the conversation right here and now. "Written guarantees are impractical," he insisted. "You can't force Rafe to protect the entire workforce, not if he plans to modernize. Changes will have to be made and once it's his company, it's well within his rights to make them."

"He's right," Ronald said with a hint of apology.

Emma glared at the two men, her pansy-blue eyes filled with determination. "Then I suggest you gentlemen come up with an idea that will reassure the townspeople. Because otherwise you're going to find all of Vista del Mar up in arms over the sale."

"Thanks to you," Chase couldn't help but point out.

She smiled sweetly in response. "My pleasure."

Chase glanced at Worth. Damn it, he could see the other man wavering, actually listening to his daughter's appeal. "Ronald, would you excuse us, so Emma and I can speak in private?"

Worth hesitated, a father's protective instincts stamped all over his face. With a reluctant jerk of his head, he opened the door. Tia stood there, a tray in hand. "Coffee?" she offered.

"Set it down on the table by the couch," Emma requested. "Dad, did you want a cup before you leave?"

Ronald snorted. "The way things are going today, I'd just spill it again. You two enjoy. I'll go sit in the kitchen and let Nilda chew off my ear for ruining two of her good tablecloths. Not to mention breaking the Wedgwood."

The instant the door closed behind Worth and Tia, Emma crossed to the tray and poured Chase a cup. She handed it to him. He promptly returned it to the tray. "A cup of coffee isn't going to hold me at a safe distance."

"Gee, and here I thought I was being polite."

His BlackBerry rang and he fished it out of his pocket. Rafe again. He sent it to voice mail and returned the phone to his pocket. When he looked at Emma, he was surprised to see laughter glittered in her eyes. "What?"

"You changed your ringtone, didn't you?"

"So? We kept getting the phones mixed up."

"I changed my ringtone, too."

He could guess where this was going and started to chuckle. "Don't tell me. Same one?"

She nodded. "Same one."

Chase held out his hand. "Come here."

To his intense satisfaction, she flung herself into his arms.

Her slight form impacted in the most delicious way. She belonged here, held close to his heart. Even better, she felt right, her curves molded against the hard angled planes of his body. He'd finally found a woman who appealed to him in every possible way and he couldn't turn around without tripping over a stumbling block. He just couldn't catch a break.

"How bad was it?" he asked gently.

"Not great." Her muffled confession came from the vicinity of his shoulder. "But not as bad as it could have been. You arrived in the nick of time."

"I should have been with you when you broke the news to your father." Chase tucked a silky lock of pale hair behind her ear and cupped her face, lifting it to his. "I know you said you'd handle it, but I should have been here, anyway."

"As it turns out, you were."

Unable to resist, he kissed her. She wrapped her arms around his waist and surrendered to the embrace. More, she encouraged it, deepening the kiss with a hungry little moan. He swept inward, shuddering at the sweetness. What would it be like to wake with her by his side every morning? To go to bed with her in his arms every night? To be there when his son or daughter came into the world and blossom from infancy to adulthood?

He'd missed out on huge chunks of that in his own life. He wouldn't allow the same thing to happen to his child. No matter what it took, he'd find a way to convince Emma that they belonged together. Reluctantly, she pulled back and glanced upward. The slumberous quality in her eyes tempted him to carry her to the couch and see what other expressions he could elicit. Only the thought of Worth walking in on them held Chase in place.

"So, what are you going to do about reassuring Worth's employees?" she asked.

He blew out a sigh. The woman had the tenacity of a bulldog and he knew just who to blame for that. "I'll bring it up with Rafe."

She rewarded him with a brilliant smile. "You do that. In the meantime, I'll work on Dad. We're all intelligent people. I'm sure we can come up with some ideas—contractual ideas—for how to protect the town."

Great. Just what he needed. How the hell was he going to get out of this one? Coming here and confronting Emma had not gone the way he'd planned. Not even a little. So much for fixing things. If anything, he'd made them worse. A hell of a lot worse.

"Focus on our upcoming nuptials, instead of Worth Industries," Chase advised as they exited the study. "Maybe if you put as much effort into that as you do the sale we might get something accomplished."

"I'm afraid our nuptials will require a few more rounds of negotiations," she replied lightly.

"I believe you were the one who said we couldn't negotiate a baby. Nor do I intend to." Ronald appeared at the far end of the foyer. Ignoring him, Chase pulled Emma into his arms and kissed her with every ounce of pent-up passion he possessed. He could practically smell the fire and brimstone pouring off her father, not that he gave a hot damn.

She reluctantly pulled back. "I won't be pressured, Chase."

"And I won't remain patient forever," he warned. "Plan on a wedding in your near future." Without another word, he exited the mansion.

His next stop was the condo Rafe recently purchased. Like the condo he rented, it also commanded a breathtaking ocean view. Unlike the rental's casual beach style, Rafe opted for something far more lavish. Rumors swirling around town put the price tag at a cool three million. Chase knew for a fact it had cost Rafe three and a half. In his opinion, the place was worth every dime.

"Well?" Rafe demanded the instant Chase arrived. "Did you take care of it? Of her?"

"No." Chase brushed past his brother and headed for the

kitchen, and more importantly, the refrigerator. He'd missed breakfast thanks to this latest fiasco and he was starving.

"What the hell do you mean, 'no'? Max has been on my ass about it all morning," Rafe said, referring to Max Preston, his high-octane corporate PR expert. "He warned this is turning into a PR nightmare and we have to fix it. Fast."

Chase opened the stainless steel door of the refrigerator and poked around, settling on a carton of leftover General Tso's chicken. He took a few minutes to stand at one of the white granite counters and eat before replying. All the while, Rafe paced the breakfast room connected to the kitchen, shooting periodic irritated looks toward his brother.

As soon as Chase had taken the edge off his appetite, he said, "I mean, Emma's not backing down. She wants some sort of guarantee that the workforce will be protected. If you were in her position, you'd be doing the same thing."

"I'm not in her position," Rafe snapped. He folded his arms across his impressive chest, a massive, immovable object to Emma's delicate, but irresistible force. "And you know damn well I'm not about to give them any guarantees. You also know why."

Chase shrugged. "Unless you want the rest of Vista del Mar to figure out your ultimate game plan, I suggest you come up with some way to reassure them. Either that or change the plan."

Rafe shook his head. "I'm not changing my plan." He stewed over the issue while Chase polished off the leftover Chinese food. "How can we keep everyone reassured long enough for me to make this buyout happen?" he asked abruptly.

"And people call me a bastard."

Rafe flashed a hard smile. "Unlike you, being called a bastard doesn't bother me."

"That's because you're not illegitimate." Chase tossed the empty carton into the trash beneath the sink and checked to make certain the area appeared as pristine as when he walked in. "You might feel differently about it if you were."

"You're probably right," Rafe conceded. "Hell, you're definitely right. At least my father married my mother when they discovered she was pregnant with me. If Dad had been any other sort of man, you and I would have even more in common than we do now."

Chase joined his brother in the breakfast area and opened the door leading onto the wraparound balcony. "Come on. I need some fresh air."

The salt-laden breeze smelled great, helping to clear his head. Rafe followed him out and the two men skirted the rattan table and chairs in favor of leaning against the railing and staring out across the magnificent view. As usual, Rafe chose only the best, and though Chase found it a bit extravagant for his tastes, the sheer beauty of the condo impressed the hell out of him and made him long for a place with substance and roots. A place overflowing with the warmth of a woman and the echoes of a child. Not just any woman or any child. Emma. Their baby. A real family. A real home.

The wish spawned the inkling of an idea that might help Rafe. Chase took a moment to weigh the possibilities before speaking. "Do you remember when my mom and your dad told us they were going to get married?"

"What I remember most is the anger and hurt. The resentment at the idea that Dad planned to replace my mother with another woman, just three short years after her death." He spared Chase a speaking look. "I also recall your beating that opinion out of me."

"Only because I knew damn well that no one could replace Hannah. I also knew that Mom wouldn't try." Chase lifted his shoulder in a shrug. "Why would she? She's a special woman in her own right."

"It took me a while to figure that out, but I got there," Rafe conceded grudgingly. "She's perfect for my dad."

A slow smile built across Chase's face. "Not as perfect as your mom, Hannah, of course."

An answering smile gentled the hard lines of his brother's

expression. "Definitely not." His sun-bleached brows drew together. "So, where are you going with this?"

"I remember Bob sitting you down—"

"Forcibly, knowing my dad."

"No doubt." Chase struggled to remember his stepfather's exact words. "Bob told you he hoped that someday you'd find a way to honor your mother so that her memory lived on. So people would always remember how special she was."

"If this is your way of trying to talk me out of my plans for Worth Industries—"

"Shut up, Rafe, and listen to me a minute. That's not what I'm getting at. You've always resented the people around here because they didn't help Hannah when she became sick. What if you started up a charity in her name, something that would keep her memory alive here in town—force people to acknowledge both her and her existence—and at the same time reassure everyone that you plan to stick around for the long haul?"

Rafe stilled, the idea clearly striking a nerve. "What sort of charity?"

"I don't know. Emma's a huge supporter of the local women's shelter, It's Time. You could throw your weight behind that."

Rafe shook his head. "No. I want something that's unique to my mother."

"Fair enough. What were her interests? Which causes was she passionate about?"

"There was one..." Rafe stared out across the ocean, a modern-day Viking at the helm of his ship. Today the waves were calm and gentle, almost like a benediction. Sunlight poured down, bouncing and glittering off the water. "She often worked with some of the Hispanic factory workers to help them improve their English skills and to teach those who couldn't, how to read. She even volunteered at the local elementary schools to work with the children who spoke English as a second language. But what mattered to her the most was adult literacy. She claimed that the only way for them to get ahead in life was through improved education and literacy. That it gave hope to the next generation. Hope for a better life than the ones their parents knew."

"Hannah's Hope?" Chase suggested softly. "Has a ring, don't you think?"

Rafe bowed his head. "Yeah, it does," he admitted gruffly.

"Get up with Max and see what he thinks about the PR possibilities."

"I'll do that."

"I have to run." Chase clapped a hand to his brother's shoulder. "You okay?"

Instantly, all hint of vulnerability vanished, disappearing behind a glacier-thick reserve. "I'm fine. But there's still the matter of Emma Worth."

"I'll worry about Emma," Chase said.

"Correction. Your job from this point forward isn't to worry about her, but to distract her. I don't care what it takes. Borrow my plane if you need to and take her someplace romantic." Rafe threw a final warning over his shoulder. "I hope you're listening, bro. Get her out of my way or I'll move her out myself."

"Ty? Ronald Worth here."

"Worth! Good to hear from you. I've been meaning to give you a call."

It was a lie. Still, Ronald would have said the same in Tiberius Barron's place. "Your son is out here working with Rafe Cameron on the purchase of my factory."

"Excellent, excellent. Glad to hear it. You couldn't have a better money man than Chase on the job."

"Right," Ronald said dryly. "Too bad he's working for the other side."

Ty chuckled. "Good point. So what's up? I assume if you're calling, there's a problem?"

"You'd be right about that. There's something I need you to straighten out."

A long pause followed. Then, "Is this regarding Chase?"

"That's right. You remember my daughter, Emma?"

"I've never had the pleasure, though you've shown me pictures. Beautiful girl, Ronald. A true credit to the Worth name."

"A true credit until your son got his hands on her."

"Son of a—" Ronald could hear a muffled crash and suspected Ty had kicked his chair aside. "What's he done now?"

"It's more a matter of what he hasn't done. Yet."

"Which is?"

"He's neglected to marry my daughter…after getting her pregnant. And I expect you to ensure he corrects that oversight as soon as possible."

Seven

Emma sat in the room set aside for practicing job interviews at It's Time, the abuse shelter where she volunteered. Three endless days had passed since she'd told her father about her pregnancy. He and Chase had spent the intervening time working on the Worth Industries sale.

Just as soon as she finished up at the shelter, she intended to join Chase for the afternoon, and she flat-out could not wait. Couldn't wait to have him hold her in his arms again or kiss her with the focused intensity that was such an innate part of his personality. Be honest, she ordered herself. She also couldn't wait for him to take her to bed again.

Emma forced her attention back to the job on hand. "That's it, Lacey." She nodded, pleased. "Your posture is fabulous. You look like a queen. No, don't look down. Keep making eye contact. Now this is the tough part. You'll have to shake hands. I'll try and make sure the HR person who interviews you is a woman, but I can't guarantee it. Try not to let it throw you if it's a man."

"I won't, Emma." Lacey lifted her chin and took a step forward, speaking in the calm, firm voice they'd practiced. "It's a pleasure to meet you."

"Excellent." Emma couldn't have been prouder. "You've done it. All these months of hard work have paid off. Your interview is at two on Monday and I don't doubt for a minute you'll get the job."

"Thanks to you."

Emma shook her head. "It's all thanks to you. You're the one who made the changes, not me. I just gave you the opportunity. And look at you now."

The two women hugged and Lacey turned to leave the room. To Emma's delight, she glowed. There was no comparison between this woman and the one who'd appeared on the shelter's doorstep, battered and bruised, her self-esteem in the toilet, unable to look people in the eye or whisper more than a few stuttered words.

Emma glanced toward the women gathered in the back of the room. She'd been warned that a delegation from Los Angeles would arrive for a visit today and, with Lacey's permission, they'd stood quietly observing while she prepared for the upcoming interview.

Emma approached the group with a welcoming smile. One of the contingent, a petite, dark-haired woman in her late fifties, stepped forward. While the others filed from the room, the woman offered her hand. "Thank you so much for allowing us to watch you."

"My pleasure. Has it helped you at all?"

"Absolutely. I particularly love the way you linked the name of the shelter, It's Time, with the name of the thrift shop, Time Again."

"Thank you. I wish I could take the credit, but one of our first residents suggested it." Emma gestured toward the doorway leading to the inner workings of the shelter. "Have you been given the grand tour?"

"Maybe this would be a good time to confess that I'm not

with the women observing you. I just sort of attached myself
to the group so I could watch you in action." Emma must have
looked confused because the woman tossed out an engaging
smile. "I'm sorry. I haven't introduced myself, have I? I'm Penny
Cameron, Chase's mother."

"Oh, dear," Emma murmured before gathering herself up. "I
mean, it's a pleasure to meet you." The polite, practiced words
sounded just like Lacey, minus the self-esteem.

Penny laughed and linked arms with her. "I'd feel the exact
same way if I were in your shoes." Her dark eyes sparkled
with undisguised mischief. "Actually, I was in your shoes
about thirty-four years ago when I discovered I was expecting
Chase."

Emma closed her eyes. "This just keeps getting better and
better."

"Chase didn't warn you he'd told me about your pregnancy,
did he?"

"Not even a little," Emma said faintly.

"Don't worry," Chase's mother reassured companionably.
"Bob and I aren't here to put any additional pressure on you.
I'm the last person in the world who'd do that."

"Rafe's dad is here, too?" she asked, dismayed.

Penny patted Emma's hand. "Don't you worry about Bob.
The only thing Rafe and his father have in common is their last
name and a deep love and respect for one another."

They joined Chase and Penny's husband, Bob Cameron, a
short time later outside the Bistro. Apprehension filled Emma.
She couldn't help but remember Chase's claim that her father
had fired Rafe's parents at a crucial juncture in their lives, when
they both needed their jobs quite desperately. Did Bob despise
her as much as he must despise her father?

Curiosity edged aside her nervousness while introductions
were made. Emma searched for some resemblance between
Rafe and his father and found very little to compare. To her
relief and delight, Bob proved to be nothing like his hard,

ruthless son, either in looks or personality. And if he felt any resentment toward her, it didn't leak into his voice or face.

Though the alpha shone like a beacon in both men, as did the sharp intelligence, she appreciated the more laid-back quality Bob exhibited and the overall kindness he portrayed. He stood right around six feet, with strong, ruggedly good-looking features and a frame of compact muscle. His graying hair remained thick, and he regarded her with direct, piercing eyes that were an interesting shade of hazel.

His quick laugh and rapid-fire wit caused her to relax after only a few minutes in his company. And the protective manner he assumed toward Penny made Emma melt a little inside. Rafe must take after his mother in both appearance and mannerisms, she concluded.

"What do you say we all head over to the street fair downtown?" Penny suggested. She swung around to face her son with a swift, birdlike motion. "Do you remember my taking you there each year when you were little?"

Chase slung an arm around his mother's shoulders, towering over her. Emma suddenly noticed that he wore jeans. She hadn't seen him so casually dressed since the morning she'd confirmed her pregnancy with a full dozen tests. He'd paired the jeans with a casual long-sleeved shirt that did drool-worthy things to the powerful expanse of his chest, as well as to an impressive set of biceps. "I loved it almost as much as you." He winked at Emma. "Her favorite part is eating her way through the fair."

"Oh, Chase. I'm not that bad."

"She's that bad," Bob confirmed. "You watch. We won't pass a single food stand she doesn't sample."

Though Penny denied it with a laugh, she proved them right by "just nipping over to grab a quick taste" of whatever delicacy the vendors offered for sale, much to everyone's amusement. Emma found the indulgent air of the two men fascinating to watch and so different from her father and his attitude toward her.

While all of Vista del Mar considered her the Worth Princess, she'd only been a princess at home so long as she remained within the tidy boundaries her father set for her. Heaven help her if she strayed too far out of her box. All hell would break loose. And how had she ended up? Pregnant and unwed. Guaranteed some psychologist somewhere would consider it a classic case of rebellion. Yet, that wasn't what she'd intended at all.

Chase waved a hand in front of her face. "Hey, you. Where'd you go?"

Emma blinked in surprise, then smiled. "Sorry. I drifted, didn't I?" She tucked her hand into the crook of Chase's arm. "I like your mom. She's..."

"Quirky?"

"Good word for it," Emma answered. "I like quirky. She's quirky and sweet and compassionate. Everything a mother should be."

"Thanks. I think so." He inclined his head toward Bob. "And my stepfather?"

She hesitated before answering, choosing her words with care. "He's not like Rafe, is he?"

"They have some things in common."

"But Bob isn't holding a grudge."

"I wouldn't put that to the test if I were you."

She paused beside a booth offering honey and homemade jellies for sale and played with one of the jars. "What do you mean?" she asked, troubled.

Chase folded his arms across his chest. The material of his shirt stretched, aligning itself to the angular dips and curves of well-toned muscle and sinew. "I mean that I don't see any holiday dinners occurring where the Worths, Camerons, Larsons and Barrons all sit down like one big, happy family. It's just not going to happen."

She tore her gaze away from the distracting expanse of brawn Chase normally kept buried beneath a suit and tie. He was right, she admitted, as much as that reality saddened her. Their son or daughter would become an instant bone of contention between warring families. "How are we going to handle the problem?"

She lowered her voice, but didn't bother to conceal her anxiety. "We can't allow all these different factions to dump their issues on our baby."

Chase lowered his voice, as well. "Don't worry, sweetheart. No one is using the baby to advance their personal agenda. I'll protect our son." He lifted a shoulder in a quick shrug. "Or our daughter."

She loved the calm certainty in his attitude. She didn't doubt for a minute that he meant what he said. She only had one question. "How? How will you stop people from using the baby?"

"Easy. If they want access to us—any of us—they'll have to cooperate."

"Even your brother?"

Chase's expression turned grim. "Especially my brother."

"It'll be interesting to see you try, if nothing else."

"Don't worry, Emma. You and our children will always come first with me."

"Our *children?* Plural?"

He didn't reply. Instead, he dropped a swift kiss on top of her head and she couldn't resist relaxing into sweet comfort. If they'd been alone and in a less public setting, she'd have offered him a more intimate kiss. Soon, she promised herself. Very soon. Because his promise filled her with a longing for something more, something permanent, to share a place with him that offered substance and roots. A place overflowing with the warmth of a man and the echoes of a child. Not just any man or any child. Chase. Their baby. A real family. A real home.

"Emma?" Penny waved to her, gesturing toward a large tent. Even with the canvas canopy, the sun sparked off of bits of gold and silver. "Come take a look at this."

Sparing Chase a quick smile that combined promise with regret, Emma joined his mother beneath the shade of the tent. Jewelry glittered from Lucite stands. "What have you found that I can't resist?" she asked with a grin.

Penny fingered a selection of bracelets. "What do you think of these?"

Emma leaned in and studied them. The bracelets were an amalgamation of beads, stones and beaten copper cut and rounded into intriguing contours that took on the shape of various animals. "I don't wear a lot of jewelry, but these are very clever. Whimsical and creative with just enough silly to make me smile."

"Do you like them?"

"I do," Emma confessed. "Particularly this one that looks like a cougar. It reminds me of Chase, of all things."

Penny nodded in agreement. "I can see why you say that. The bits of lapis lazuli match his eyes and it has his lithe, muscular shape, doesn't it?"

"I think I'm offended," Chase muttered. He glanced over his shoulder at Bob. "Am I offended at being compared to a bracelet?"

"Definitely."

"Okay, yes. I'm offended."

Emma waved him silent and continued to debate the merits with Penny. "These shouldn't be my style, if you know what I mean. But they are."

"Why aren't they your style? Too offbeat? Not worthy of a Worth?"

Emma chuckled at the teasing note in Penny's voice and assumed her haughtiest tone of voice. "Certainly not. A Worth only wears diamonds or gold." She dropped the act and lifted the bracelet off the rack. "No, I meant I wasn't sure I could do it justice. That I could wear it with the sort of flair it deserves. But I really do like it."

"Well, I think the bracelet suits you," Penny insisted stoutly, "and that you have more than enough flair to pull it off."

"You've convinced me." Emma opened her purse and pulled out her wallet. "I'm going to take it."

"Put that away. I'd like to buy it for you," Penny offered.

Emma drew back. "Oh, no, I can't let you do that. I'm happy to pay for it myself."

"You're carrying my grandchild." It was said so quietly, so gently. "Please let me buy this for you. It's a small thing and not very expensive. And it would make me very happy."

Emma softened. "Of course. Thank you." She slipped the bracelet onto her wrist and admired it. "I really do love it."

"Of course you do. I'm sure I must have made it with you in mind. I just didn't realize it until we met."

Emma froze. "What?"

Penny chuckled. "I'm afraid I set you up. I make these bracelets in my spare time and have a friend who sells them at the various fairs and tradeshows. Here, I'll show you." She turned Emma's arm to show her the copper penny that had been beaten and shaped into the catch. "I use pennies as my signature."

"Oh," Emma said faintly. "I guess it's a good thing I said I liked your bracelets."

Penny shrugged. "If you hadn't, I wouldn't have dreamed of embarrassing you by admitting I'd made them." She smiled warmly. "But I had a feeling they'd catch your fancy. And, as a matter of fact, I made the one you're wearing with Chase in mind."

"Then I'm thrilled it's the one I chose." She gave Penny a quick hug. "Thank you for giving it to me. I'll treasure it even more knowing you made it."

The four of them continued on their way and Chase glanced down at Emma. "You okay?" he asked, taking her hand in his.

It felt good to have him hold her hand, his strength communicated through that simple act. "I'm fine. I feel like I just escaped a minefield, though."

"You didn't. Seriously. Mom wouldn't have been offended, even if you hated the bracelet. She's really laid-back about stuff like that." He lifted an eyebrow. "Did you really like it or were you being polite?"

"I love it," she said with absolute sincerity. "I was serious when I said I didn't think I'd do it justice."

"Sweetheart, you could wear Tarzan's loincloth and make it work."

Her mouth quivered. "Tarzan's loincloth? Not Jane's?"

"Definitely Tarzan's. And the bracelet." He shot her a hungry look. "Or maybe just the bracelet."

After another delightful hour together, the two couples parted, Bob claiming they had a long drive home. "We took the coast road on the way here," Penny informed them. She nudged Chase with her elbow. "I saw a place just north of Busted Bluff with an open house sign. You and Emma should check it out. Remember how we used to play the game?"

"Sure. If we find time, Emma and I will drop by."

She waited until his parents left before regarding him with a lifted eyebrow. "Was that a suggestion that we find a place and move in together, or did she really mean a game?"

"She really meant a game."

Intriguing. "How do you play?"

He stopped by a vendor on the outskirts of the street fair and bought them each an ice cream cone. She could see him debating how much to explain. "We didn't have a lot of money during those early years," he admitted. "Mom refused to accept any support from my father. Or to be exact, she refused the strings that went along with the money. So, after church on Sunday, wearing our one good outfit, we would stop by open houses and pretend."

"Pretend?" She didn't understand. "Pretend...what?"

"Pretend that we could afford to buy the house we toured. We'd talk about where we'd put our furniture or what changes we'd make." He smiled reminiscently. "We'd spend that hour fantasizing about what it would be like to live in a big, fancy house."

"It's not always what it's cracked up to be," Emma murmured.

Chase leaned in and kissed a smear of ice cream from her

chin. "No, it's not. But those childhood fantasies are part of what gave me the drive to succeed in life."

"And to exchange fantasy for reality?"

"Of course."

She eyed him shrewdly. "For you? Or for your mother?"

"It didn't hurt that I could give Mom all the material things she couldn't afford when I was little. For a while it got to be a competition between me and Rafe. Who could give the bigger, more outrageous gift to our parents."

"I'll bet your mother and Bob didn't let that go on for long."

"Nope. They finally told us the only gift they'd accept from either of us was the gift of our time."

"That's so sweet." Emma gave serious attention to her ice-cream cone while she framed her next question. "Do you suppose going to open houses would be as much fun now that you're older and can actually afford any house you toured?"

"I don't know. I guess we'll find out."

Startled, she looked at him. "Find out?"

"Do you have other plans?"

"No." Emma considered, then nodded. Why not? "Sounds like fun."

Well, maybe *fun* wasn't the right word, Emma decided when she stepped across the threshold of the open house. Mind-boggling. That would be one word she'd use. Eye-popping. That would be another. Some crazed decorator had taken a nice, solid home with excellent flow, light and balance, and had deliberately done their best to crush it beneath the most opulent and garish furnishings she'd ever seen.

"I can't seem to wrap my head around it," she whispered to Chase. "My eyes won't settle on anything."

"Mine are settling on everything and I think my head's going to explode."

"There's something else, though…" She wandered into the living room and paused on the threshold. Someone had stuffed far too much oversized furniture into far too small a space.

"Something almost familiar about the place. I just can't put my finger on it."

"You've been to a bordello?" he asked politely.

She struggled to control a laugh, unwilling to attract anyone's attention. Bordello. It perfectly described the gold-and-red wallpaper stamped with black velvet fleurs-de-lis. "I have now," she murmured.

"Do you have any questions I can answer?" A woman in her sixties appeared behind them. She smiled in a friendly fashion. "I'm Mrs. Strickland, the owner."

Chase stuck out his hand. "Pleased to meet you. My fiancée and I were just commenting that we've never seen anything like this before."

The older woman beamed. "Oh, well. I tried."

Emma felt a sinking sensation in the pit of her stomach. Suddenly, it didn't seem so funny, anymore. She glanced at Chase and gave him a worried look, hoping he wouldn't say anything insensitive. He noted her concern and nodded to let her know he'd caught the silent message. "You decorated this yourself?"

"I did, though I can't take all the credit. I duplicated a magazine layout of the Worth estate." The woman examined her living room with intense satisfaction. "Everything you see here is exactly what they have. So, if you buy the house, you'll be living in the same luxurious comfort as the Worth family."

"Oh." Emma stiffened in dawning horror. "Oh, my. You're right."

"You saw the layout? You must have been very young since it's been years ago now." The woman stepped forward and ran her hand along the back of the sofa in an affectionate manner. "This is identical to the one the Worths own. All the furniture is. I simply improved on it a little. Tweaked some of the duller bits."

"Duller bits?" Emma repeated weakly.

"The late Mrs. Worth liked more neutral colors. Surprising, considering she was an artist. I decided to brighten it up a bit."

She leaned in and lowered her voice. "A vast improvement if you ask me."

They allowed the woman to take them on an extended tour of the house, proudly showing them all the improvements she'd made so that her standard of living matched or exceeded the Worths. Once she satisfied herself that they'd seen every detail the house had to offer, they returned to the car.

"Well, that didn't go quite as planned," Chase observed.

Shell-shocked, Emma slid into the passenger seat. "No, not at all."

"Are those the same furnishings that are out at your dad's?"

"When my mother was alive, yes. Not anymore, thank God. We've remodeled over the years. Otherwise I'd have to gut the entire estate."

He glanced at her in concern. "Are you all right?"

She took a deep breath. "To be honest, I don't know whether to laugh or cry."

"You're lucky she didn't recognize you."

"Very, though I do try to stay out of the limelight. I'm not often photographed these days, so that probably helped."

He reached for her hand, laced her fingers with his own. "I'm sorry, sweetheart. That was supposed to be fun and instead I'm afraid it bordered on creepy."

Emma waved his comment aside. "I'm not concerned about that part. I just feel terrible for that poor woman."

"Why?" Chase asked in surprise. "She loved her home. You could tell she didn't want to sell it, just as you could tell she spent many wonderful years living in a home every bit as grand and beautiful as the Worths."

"More beautiful," Emma reminded him.

"An improved version."

They looked at each other and burst out laughing. She rested her head against his shoulder and grinned. It felt marvelous to simply kick back, relax and act a little silly. So much had happened in the past few months, much of it stressful, that she'd forgotten how to enjoy herself.

Until Chase.

Even though he epitomized the driven businessman, he still knew how to play. He'd demonstrated that on the first day they'd met, when they'd treated New York City like their private playground. She studied him, caught the edginess evident in the taut set of his jaw and the sharp intelligence in his smoky blue eyes. There sat the financier.

She also noted the lines that fanned out from the corner of those eyes and the easy curve of a mouth she'd taken great delight in kissing. A mouth quick to smile, a man quick to laugh. A protective man. An honorable one. She found the combination irresistible.

"What?" He'd caught her staring.

"Just trying to figure you out."

"What's your conclusion?"

"I'm not sure, yet." She hesitated. "You were so kind to Mrs. Strickland."

"Did you expect me to be cruel?"

"No, of course not." She swiveled to face him. "But she made a mess of that house. She chose completely inappropriate furnishings and then added to the disaster with her color choices, all so she could imitate my family's lifestyle. I don't understand that, especially since her perception of the Worths is about as far from reality as it could get. And yet, as you pointed out, you could tell how happy her home made her."

"There's no accounting for taste or what will make people happy."

"No, there isn't. Clearly, she loved the fantasy she created. That doesn't change the fact that you were so gentle with her when you could have been sarcastic. She wouldn't have caught on. It would have gone right over her head."

"That's not who I am."

"No," Emma murmured. "I can see that."

He lifted an eyebrow. "Did you think I was?"

"Not really." She fastened her seat belt with a satisfied smile. "Today you proved it."

He started the car and continued along the coast road to a section where the homes became mansions sitting on several acres of property. Balloons marked another open house and on impulse, Emma pointed to it. "Stop there. I'll bet you'd normally have to make an appointment to tour that place. Let's take a look. Do you mind?"

"You really are a glutton for punishment."

"Think of it as cleansing your palette after eating something bitter."

"Okay, but don't get your hopes up."

The two of them entered the house. The difference was so dramatic that they both heaved a sigh of relief, then laughed at their identical reaction. "Now pay attention to how it's done," he murmured.

"You're the expert."

He draped an arm around her shoulder and pulled her close. Her hip and thigh bumped up against his and she couldn't stop herself from surrendering to his warmth. Not when he felt this incredible. It suddenly occurred to her that he hadn't kissed her yet today and she missed those moments of passion more than she could have believed possible.

He must have read something in her face because a hint of desire drifted across his expression and settled in his gaze. "Tonight," he said, and she wondered if he meant it as a threat or a promise.

A real estate agent greeted them, handing out literature detailing information about the property, including the multimillion-dollar price sticker. "Feel free to wander. I'm showing another party through, but I'll be around if you have any questions."

They started with the living room. "See, now this is a terrific room. Nice flow," Chase commented. "Our living room set would fit perfectly."

Emma blinked. "It would?" He gave her a swift hip nudge and she caught on. "Oh, right. It would."

"I love the stone fireplace. Put a couple of chairs there and we could read in front of the fire."

Emma shook her head. "A love seat would work better. That way we could curl up together with a glass of wine and a good book."

He feathered a kiss along the curve of her cheek. "See? You're a natural."

Actually, she'd been serious. "Why don't we check out the kitchen? Nilda worked very hard to teach me to cook and I'd like something worthy of my truly unfortunate skills."

"That bad?"

"Oh, yeah."

"Does it have a refrigerator? That's all I care about."

Emma couldn't prevent a laugh. Then she stepped into the kitchen and sighed. "Oh, Chase. It's a gourmet kitchen."

"Gourmet?"

"It has all the extras." She pointed. "A grill, a warming drawer under the oven, a faucet over the stove, a walk-in pantry and wine cellar."

"Not to mention an industrial-size refrigerator." Chase nodded in satisfaction. "I'll bet that'll keep my beer cold."

She waved him silent. "Look at the terra-cotta backsplash. It's modern and yet has that Italian-farmhouse feel to it, don't you think?"

"You're even better at this than my mother," he informed her in an undertone.

He still thought she was playacting. She sighed. "There's a pretty breakfast room." She wandered in that direction. "I like how it has a view of the water."

"Do you want to tour the upstairs?"

"I really would."

She trailed behind him, admiring the wood trim and expert craftsmanship. Everything about the house appealed. It offered the beauty and lightness she craved and the sophistication better suited to Chase's New York palate. She couldn't have found a better blend of their two tastes if she'd designed the place herself.

"Check this out, Emma."

She turned to discover that Chase had wandered down the lengthy upstairs hall of the south wing and into one of the rooms there. She joined him, inhaling sharply. "A his-and-her office."

The two rooms were identical, each with its own gas fireplace and doors that opened onto a shared balcony. Etched glass pocket doors could be opened so that the two rooms became one, or shut for privacy. The current owners had a pair of desks positioned opposite the doors, one in each room, hers a dainty French provincial in cherry and his a more substantial piece carved from mahogany.

Chase stilled. "They're facing each other."

"So they can see one another while they work." For some reason, tears threatened and Emma crossed to the balcony door while she struggled to regain her equilibrium. "And look at this. The deck doesn't connect to any of the others around the house. They have complete privacy."

"Did you notice the table and chairs?" He came to stand behind her, resting his hands on her shoulders. "I'll bet they go out there at lunchtime and eat together."

She leaned into his embrace. "Or share a glass of wine while they watch the sunset." She sighed. "I wonder why they're giving up such a magnificent place?"

He gestured toward a cane resting in the corner. "Maybe the steps have become too much for one of them. A shame, really. It's a beautiful home."

Her heart went out to the owners. "Yes, it is." The kind of home she'd choose for herself.

He must have read her mind. "Why don't you have your own place?"

She shrugged, hoping he didn't pick up in the tension that

gathered in the muscles beneath his hands. "No point. Not with that huge estate standing practically empty."

"I don't suppose it has anything to do with the fact that if you moved out it would leave your father all alone on that huge estate?"

"That might play some small part in my decision," she admitted.

"It's going to happen, Emma, and soon."

"You're assuming too much." She pulled free of his hold. "We haven't decided to marry. And if we don't, it makes sense for me to live with our son or daughter in the home where I grew up."

"Not a chance."

She swung around to face him. "Why not? It's a reasonable solution."

"No, the reasonable solution is to marry and for the three of us to live together as a family."

"In New York? In your apartment? I mean, it's nice. But it's not where I'd choose to raise a family," she objected.

He hesitated. "Would it influence your decision to marry me if I said I'd be willing to shift my base of operations to Vista del Mar?"

It took a moment for his offer to penetrate. "You'd actually consider that?" she asked in an odd voice.

"Yes, I would. I have zero interest in being a long-distance parent. If you're adamant about remaining in California, then I'm willing to consider moving out here."

She hesitated, then approached, surprising them both by wrapping her arms around his neck. "I don't know what this is between us…." She hesitated, attempting to put words to the confusing jumble of emotions racing through her. "Whether there's something more between us than just a baby."

"You're right. There is."

"Maybe so. All I know for certain is that I'd like to find out." Truth time. She refused to give him false hope or false expectations. "I'm not ready to marry you, Chase, not even to

give our child the legal right to your name. I can tell you that
I won't marry you for that sake alone. But the fact that you're
willing to move here in order to establish a relationship with
our baby—"

"And with you."

A slow smile lit her face. "I'd like that, Chase. I'd like that
very much."

He leaned down, his mouth hovering above hers. "Shall we
make it official?" he asked, his eyes gleaming with laughter.

She planted a hand on his chest to hold him at bay. Taut
muscles rippled beneath her fingers. "Is this how you make
all your deals official?" she asked. "That's a rather peculiar
investment firm you're running."

"Only with you, sweetheart. Only with you."

And then he kissed her.

Eight

Instantly, Emma fell into Chase's embrace, lost to their surroundings. She couldn't get enough of him. He tasted so incredible, while the restless stroke of his hands drove her emotions into a total frenzy. She'd been raised to be polite and calm and poised even in the most egregious of circumstances. Yet, Chase managed to utterly decimate that ability.

When had she become so vulnerable to his touch, so completely open and defenseless? She could guess when. The seeds were planted the first time they were together, when she'd discovered that a single night didn't come close to satisfying her. And how had she handled it? She'd run. She never dreamed that he'd find her again. Or that more seeds had taken root that night than an emotional susceptibility to him.

Her fingers slid deep into his crisp dark blond hair and she anchored him close, opening to him and allowing all that was most intensely feminine respond to all that was most imperatively male. She had the sneaking suspicion that if they'd been anywhere else, their clothes would have long since disappeared and they'd have made the rug their bed. Instead, he reluctantly pulled back.

"Emma."

"No," she murmured, wanting more. Needing more. "Not yet."

"I know, sweetheart, but someone's coming."

She stiffened within his arms, hearing them for the first time. The sound of their voices came from a few feet away. She'd been deaf to their approach, so lost in Chase's embrace that she didn't doubt for a moment the real estate agent and prospective buyers would have walked in on a moment of explosive passion if Chase hadn't come to his senses.

With a soft gasp, she ripped free of his arms and crossed swiftly to the doors leading onto the balcony. Exiting the house, she stood at the railing, her arms wrapped around her waist. She stared out across the water and dragged air into her lungs like a woman drowning.

Control. She needed to regain her self-control. But deep down she knew that when it came to Chase, she asked the impossible. She forced herself to straighten and tuck her blouse into her slacks. Then she smoothed the collar of the cropped jacket she wore. The wind tossed her hair, adding to the tangles their embrace had created. Nothing she could do about that. Finally, she opened her purse and removed her lipstick and compact and outlined the swollen contours of her bare mouth.

A moment later, Chase joined her, closing the door behind them to protect their privacy from the party being escorted through the house. "I don't understand any of this," she informed Chase without turning around. She snapped her compact closed and tossed it and the tube of lipstick into her purse. "I don't know how to handle it."

"Don't try," he advised.

"Whatever is going on with me must be hormonal. It's the only explanation."

"Is it?"

Something in his tone had her spinning around. "What else

could it be?" Tears threatened again. "If it's not hormones, that leaves lust or love. Take your pick."

He thrust his hands into his trouser pockets and leaned against the frame of the door. "Is it important to define what we're feeling at this point?"

"It would help," she retorted defensively.

He looked out across the water, much as she'd done. "This house is perfect, you know."

He'd changed the subject. Or maybe he hadn't. Maybe he attacked it from a different angle. She glanced around, taking in house, grounds and ocean. Her throat closed over. "It is perfect, isn't it?"

"I can see us living here." He shot her a smile that turned her insides liquid. "I can see us sharing that office. You could work on your paperwork for the shelter and the thrift shop while I did the same for Larson Investments."

His comment threw her off balance. "Your firm isn't a one-man operation, is it? Wouldn't you want an actual office downtown, with staff to run it?"

He shrugged. "Sure. But that doesn't mean I have to go in every day, especially after the baby's born."

She stared at him, stumbling to keep up with the flow of the conversation. For some reason, she couldn't quite grasp the implications. "I… You would stay home?" The concept seemed so foreign she couldn't wrap her brain around it. "With the baby?"

He raised his shoulders in a casual shrug. "Of course with the baby. If you need to put some hours in at the shelter, I don't see why it would be a problem for me to watch Junior. We'd have to arrange our schedules around feedings and juggle who goes into the office when. I'm sure there'll be the occasional work conflict. But with a little consideration and cooperation, we'll manage."

"My…my father practically lived at the office," she said, her voice faltering.

It was the wrong thing to say. Chase's expression darkened.

He straightened from his stance and approached. "Let's get something clarified right up front. I am not, nor will I ever be, like either your father or my own. And I strongly urge you to never attempt to compare me to either of them again."

She lifted her chin. "You can't deny certain similarities."

He snagged that aggressive little chin and leaned in. "All men have a few things in common, as do all women. Other than that, I prefer to be judged on my own merits. In case you haven't noticed, if I were anything like my father, I wouldn't be here. I wouldn't for one tiny moment consider moving my base of operations to Vista del Mar. And I sure as hell wouldn't be standing on this balcony with you, seriously tempted to write out a check for this house, here and now."

Emma's heart gave an odd tug. "Are you serious?"

"Dead serious. I would like to take a look at the master bedroom suite and make certain there's a suitable room for the nursery. But other than that, this place is perfect for both of us and you know it. It might as well have been built with both our tastes in mind."

His comment matched her earlier thoughts. Longing welled up, threatening to overflow and spill out in great, messy waves. He'd seen it, too. All this time she'd thought him oblivious to how beautifully suited they were to this home and how well it conformed to their needs. Instead, he'd taken it all in and recognized it for what it was. Perfection. She should have known. Chase missed very little. Even so, to buy a house of this magnitude on a whim. On a chance. On a dream that might never become reality...

"Oh, Chase," she whispered. "Please don't do this. Not if it's just an attempt to convince me to marry you."

He fisted his hands on his hips. "Give me one good reason why I shouldn't."

"That's just it. I don't have any good reasons," she confessed. "And that terrifies me."

He reached for her, pulled her into warmth and passion and promises of a glittering future. "Take a chance, Emma."

"Not marriage, Chase. I can't agree to that. Not yet."

"Then agree to the house. Agree to move in with me while we make our decision. If it doesn't work out, you can always return to the estate."

She closed her eyes, fighting the temptation with all she possessed. But she couldn't. She wanted the dream. Taking a deep breath, she leaped, praying she would fly instead of hurtle to the ground.

"Okay, let's do it."

The next week passed in an endless round of meetings that kept Chase busier than he would have liked. Inch by excruciating inch, they drew closer to finalizing the sale of Worth Industries to Rafe. Hour after excruciating hour they hammered out a contract filled with ifs, ands and buts that required the lawyers to pick apart every word. All the while Chase's team of accountants put in countless time figuring out how each addendum and change would affect the bottom line.

At the end of one particularly grueling session, Rafe approached Chase. "Lucky you. Your part in all this is almost over."

Chase scrubbed his face in exhaustion. Hell, he needed a shave. Again. "I couldn't be that lucky. Why is Worth dragging his feet? Every time I turn around he's trying to shove another change into the contract."

Rafe thrust a hand through his pale hair. "And every time he shoves in another change, my team of lawyers runs up more fees picking them back out again. It's nothing new. You know that. He's stalling because this is his baby. And on some level he may suspect what I'm about to do." Rafe's expression hardened. "Not that it's going to stop me."

"You haven't changed your mind on that front?"

"Not even a little." He lowered his voice. "Which brings me to what I need from you."

"Name it."

"Get Emma out of town. I have a feeling we're going to wrap this thing up over the weekend and it would help if she wasn't around to cause any last-minute trouble."

"As it turns out, I won't have to get her out of town. She's already going."

Some of the edginess eased from Rafe's voice. "That's the first piece of good news I've heard all day. Where's she going?"

"We. We're going."

Rafe considered. "That won't be a problem. Like I said, your job is just about through." He folded his arms across his chest. "Is it a secret or are you planning to share?"

"We're going to San Francisco."

"Nice."

"Not so nice. Some little bird dropped the news in The Barron's ear that Emma's pregnant." Chase shot a disgruntled glare in the direction of the conference room. "I can guess who. Anyway, the great man himself is flying in to check on some office building he's constructing and he's ordered us to make a command appearance."

Rafe laughed. "Tell you what, feel free to take my jet up to San Francisco. So long as Emma is out of the picture and not running her mouth to reporters—"

Chase stiffened. "Careful," he warned.

The quiet forcefulness of his tone got through to Rafe where anger wouldn't have. "Seriously?" He made an impatient sound. "Okay, I can see you're dead serious. Damn it, Chase. It's gotten to the point where I can't talk to you at all, anymore."

"You can talk to me. You just need to stop making derogatory comments about my future wife and the mother of my child."

"Hell."

Chase slapped his brother on the shoulder. "It's rough, but I have confidence in you. You'll get the hang of it."

"Whatever you say." He bared his teeth. "Give your father my best regards."

Chase winced. "That was low, even for you."

"My pleasure." Rafe checked his watch. "Come on, bro. Let's get back in there and find out what Worth has tried to sneak by my sharks in the last five minutes."

The next few days flew by and as the weekend approached the deal teetered on the edge of completion. They were well past the point of no return, Chase decided, satisfied. Not that he'd mention as much to Emma. If her father elected to say something, that was his choice. Discretion appealed far more, particularly when it came to his bride-to-be, and particularly since she still needed more convincing to go from bride-to-be to done deal.

At long last, Saturday morning dawned bright and clear and the flight to San Francisco in Rafe's luxurious business jet proved uneventful. A car waited to transport them into the city. It couldn't have gone any smoother. For some reason it made Chase wonder at what point the weekend would all go hideously wrong.

At a guess, the minute Tiberius Barron entered the picture.

"Where are we meeting your father?" Emma asked, proving once again that she possessed an uncanny knack for reading his mind.

"He has a building under construction downtown. We're to join him there."

She paused and he could tell she chose her words with care. "We're meeting him at a construction site?"

"I believe the actual construction phase is complete. They're working on the finishing touches." He offered a cool smile. "My father is a man who believes in multitasking."

"So I gather." She touched the bracelet she wore with a troubled expression. It was the one his mother had designed and purchased for Emma. Noticing her attachment to it filled Chase with fierce pleasure. "He can't spare time to sit down over lunch or even a cup of coffee and talk?"

"My father is a busy man."

"I see."

She didn't say anything more for a long time, but Chase could tell she was mulling over his words. He could practically see the bullet points she busily created, an entire relentless row of the nasty little suckers. She would connect the dots from this point onward until he wouldn't be able to take any more and snapped.

He didn't want to snap. Not at Emma. He steeled himself against the coming conversation. Being the thorough, detail-oriented sort, she started with dot number one.

"Has your father always been this busy?" she asked.

"I never saw much of him growing up," he explained, pleased with the mildness of his response.

"Why not? You were living with him."

"No, actually I wasn't."

She released a sigh of exasperation. "I'm sorry. Maybe the baby is using up all my brain cells, but I really don't understand any of this. I thought you went to live with your father when you were ten." And here came dot number two, dropping with a splat, like a gift from the back end of a seagull. "How could you live with him and not see him?"

Damn. He really didn't want to get into this. Not now. He'd hoped, not ever. Foolish to think Emma wouldn't ask at some point. "The same way you never saw your brother after the age of fifteen. I arrived in New York and was immediately shipped off to prep school. Living with my father was just a euphemism for being under his control and having my upbringing orchestrated by him."

"Oh, Chase! That's appalling."

He shrugged. "That's The Barron for you."

"And when you weren't at school? Where did you go?"

"Our…agreement, I guess you'd call it, permitted me to spend my summers and holidays with Mom." He reflected on the conclusion he'd reached long ago regarding that particular arrangement. "No doubt because my stepmother, Karis, wanted nothing to do with me. Understandable, I suppose."

Emma stared at Chase in utter disbelief. "Are you telling

me The Barron took you away from Penny and then ignored you? Why would he do that? It doesn't make any sense."

He smiled at the way she'd picked up his habit of referring to his father as "The Barron" while dodging the third dot with impressive dexterity. "You'd have to ask him."

Emma lifted an eyebrow. "Will he be any more forthcoming than you?"

"Doubtful."

"Got it." There was a significant pause while she strolled over to dot number four and gave it a good, swift kick. "Was your father married at the time you were conceived?" she asked. "Is that why your stepmother wanted nothing to do with you?"

"I believe he was engaged to Karis at the time." He hoped like hell they arrived at the site soon. Damn soon. Before they reached the next dot.

Emma winced. "Ouch. How many Barron stepbrothers and sisters do you have?"

Too late for a timely rescue. She's reached dot number five, the most telling one of all. "Karis has never had any children. I could never think of a polite way to ask why, since I guarantee my father wanted sons. Legitimate sons, that is."

"Ah."

He turned a disgruntled look on her. "What does 'ah' mean?"

"It means I understand."

"Excellent. No more dots."

Her brows pulled together in confusion. "Excuse me?"

"I mean, we can finally put this conversation to rest."

"Forever more?" she probed delicately.

"I couldn't be that lucky."

"I suspect you're right, but I do sympathize. After all, I'm just as touchy about the subject of my mother's death. Not to mention the estrangement from my brother."

"Then you'll leave it alone?"

"Mmm."

He swore beneath his breath. "Let me put it this way. You will leave it alone."

"Oh, look." She pointed out the window at an impressive high-rise. "I think that must be the building."

"What gave it away?"

She grinned. "Maybe the sign that says Future Home of Barron's West."

He couldn't resist her smile. He pulled her close and gave her a slow, thorough kiss. She responded with unstinting generosity, her curves fitting against him as though tailor-made. Slowly his hand crept downward and his fingers splayed across her abdomen.

Their child rested there. He craved these moments when he could touch that precious bundle tucked so snugly within her womb. To try to sense the baby's presence through the protective layers of flesh and bone. More than anything, he wanted to strip away her clothes and press his lips against the softening mound of her belly. To rest his cheek there and pretend he could hear the rapid whoosh of his baby's heartbeat or feel the flutter of its first movements.

Her name escaped in a whisper. "Emma…"

She pulled back slightly and traced the curve of his jaw with a tender touch. Gathering her hand in his, she pressed a little tighter and cupped her hands over his. "Still there, safe and sound."

He lowered his voice, as though to keep from disturbing the baby's slumber. "Has he…she…moved, yet?"

"I haven't felt anything. From what I've read that won't happen for another few weeks."

He rested his forehead against hers. "Will you tell me when it happens?"

"You'll be the first to know, I promise."

The car pulled to a stop and the driver climbed from his seat. It gave them just enough time to straighten and smooth and collect themselves. An instant later, the door opened beside Emma. She sent Chase an encouraging smile before exiting the car. The minute he joined her, she took his hand in hers, uniting them as a couple. As they approached, he could feel the critical gaze of his father and stepmother from where they stood in the shadow of the huge building. He wondered if Emma felt it, too. If so, had she taken his hand for protection...or to protect? Maybe he'd ask her when they were next alone.

The introductions were brief, formal and bitterly cold. Though Karis greeted Emma with some degree of warmth, she avoided looking at him. As usual. Chase and his father shook hands with brisk, distant efficiency. Then his stepmother swept Emma in one direction while his father ushered him in the other. He could hear Karis inviting Emma to go shopping and was amused to see the invitation blown off, much to his stepmother's irritation.

"Are you listening to me?" Tiberius Barron demanded.

"Yes. You were asking about a wedding date. Nothing has been set."

"Why not?"

"It's quite simple. The lady in question hasn't agreed to marry me."

The Barron's eyes, the same smoky blue shade as his own, ignited with temper. "Now you listen to me, boy. Emma is a Worth. She's a Smith graduate. Her pedigree is impeccable. And she's clearly fertile, which means legitimate children, something I've never been fortunate enough to possess."

Huh. One of Emma's dots just got connected to the others. He'd have to let her know. "I realize how lucky I am to have her. Maybe my mongrel status doesn't appeal to her," he admitted humbly. He contemplated the possibility. "Now that I think about it, marrying me would be a step down for her."

"Don't be ridiculous. You have Barron blood running through your veins, even if it's been diluted."

Chase stiffened. "Diluted or polluted?" he asked very, very softly.

Ty waved that aside. "Don't be fatuous. You know damn well what I'm talking about." His crisp, hard words shot out like bullets. "Emma Worth isn't some cheap piece of goods you can fool around with and then walk away from. You can't skip out on your obligations and responsibilities to her so easily."

A haze of red settled across Chase's vision, interfering with his ability to think and speak with his usual calm control. "Let me get this straight. I should shoulder my obligations and responsibilities—in other words, marry Emma because she's pregnant. But you never felt obligated to do the same thing for Mom?" It was a question he'd longed to ask ever since he'd first learned the facts of his birth.

Barron smoldered. "Your mother wasn't the kind of woman you marry."

Chase froze, his hands balling into fists. Before he could use them, Emma approached and forced his fingers apart, interlacing them with hers. He caught a brief glimpse of Karis's rigid back as she exited the site and climbed into the limo waiting to whisk her off to the shopping district.

"What have I missed?" Emma asked lightly.

"Nothing," both men said in unison.

"Funny." She fixed The Barron with an icy look. "I could have sworn I heard you tell your son that his mother wasn't the sort of woman worthy of marriage."

Dull color swept along Ty's cheekbones. "Excuse me. I was attempting to protect your interests against my son's carelessness."

"My interests?" She lifted an eyebrow in polite inquiry. "Or your own?"

Aw, hell. "Let it go, Emma," Chase advised.

She glanced down and for an instant he thought the moment would blow over. Then she touched the bracelet encircling her wrist—his mother's bracelet—and her head jerked up. "No. I don't think I will let it go."

"You have something to say to me, Ms. Worth?" Ty used his most intimidating tone of voice, not that it fazed Emma one iota.

"I have a great deal to say to you, Mr. Barron." Fire burned in her gaze, along with an intense anger. A protective anger. One stirred by her feelings for him, Chase realized with a sense of wonder. "You pressured a ten-year-old boy into deserting his mother in order to live with you."

"Nonsense."

She swept aside The Barron's interruption as though it held little or no merit. Which, Chase conceded, it didn't. "And once you had your son in your clutches, you dumped him into a prep school where he was subjected to unimaginable ridicule and torment because you chose to allow him to come into this world a bastard."

"A marriage to Penny Larson would have been a disaster."

"Then why didn't you formally adopt Chase?" It was a devastating question, one that Chase had never dared ask, mainly because he didn't want to know the answer. Or maybe he knew the answer and would rather not hear it put into actual words. "You couldn't even be troubled to give him the protection of your name, could you?" She stepped closer, invading The Barron's territory. "Why? Why would you do that?"

She'd actually shaken the old man. Ty shook his head, avoiding her gaze. "That's none of your business."

Her voice lowered, intensified. "Well, let me tell you something, Mr. Barron. I have a very good idea why. Don't for one moment think I haven't figured it out. All you cared about were your own self-interest. When I think of that poor child…"

She broke off and her fingers curled over the tiny mound of her belly in an instinctive gesture, a distinctly maternal gesture of protection that forged a connection in Chase's mind between the boy he'd been and the child she carried. To his distress, tears filled her eyes and her mouth trembled. Before he could step in and put an end to the conversation, she pressed her lips together into a firm line and forced past the tears.

"You never gave a single thought to the feelings of your own son. You never once armored him against the cruelty with which society regarded him. Not with your name. Not with your love." She drew in a swift, trembling breath. "You should be ashamed of yourself. I know I am."

With that, Emma turned into Chase's embrace and burst into tears. He wrapped her up in a protective hold. "I believe that's my signal to rescue the damsel in distress from the ferocious dragon."

"I think I'm the one who needs rescuing," Ty growled, his complexion pasty white. "In fact, I know I am."

"We'll be going now, in case you hadn't picked up on that fact. Nice seeing you as always, Dad. Give our best regards to Karis."

"Chase, I..." For the first time in his entire life, Chase witnessed his father groping for words. "I...I'm sorry, son. For everything. I never looked at any of this from a child's point of view. Until now, that is. Until Emma."

A fierce pride swept through Chase. "She has a way with words, doesn't she?"

"You might say that." Ty closed his eyes. "Listen to me, Chase. You have the chance to do what I never would. I hope you handle your choices better than I have. Maybe when Emma is feeling better—" He stumbled to a halt. "I'd like to make amends. To both of you."

"I'll see what I can do."

"He can come to the wedding," Emma sobbed. "If there is a wedding."

Ty hesitated, uncertain how to respond. "I'll be there," he said at last. "Assuming there is a there."

Chase figured they weren't going to resolve their differences any better than that. Not today, at any rate. Without another word, he carried Emma back to the waiting car. "Where to?" the driver asked.

"Sweetheart?"

She wiped her eyes. "Would you mind if we just went home?"

"No, of course not."

He didn't know if Emma realized it, yet, but with that single

blazing speech, she'd just fully and completely committed
herself to him. If she didn't, she soon would. He'd make sure
of that. Because she'd given him the one thing he'd never had
and always craved.

A home.

"Take us to the airport," he instructed.

Dear God, a home. His arms tightened around Emma. Even
better, it was a home they'd share together.

Nine

Emma spared Chase a swift look and winced. For the past several hours he'd been lost in his own thoughts, barely speaking a word the entire flight back to San Diego. She could only assume she'd said far too much to his father. Regret filled her. Granted, Chase had been kindness itself, making certain she wanted for nothing once they were aboard Rafe's jet, helping her on the plane in San Francisco and off again in San Diego, holding her car door. But, he'd reverted to type. And it wasn't a type she cared for.

At all.

During the drive from the airport, her BlackBerry made a soft *burring* noise indicating an incoming call. Chase reached into his pocket and tossed her his phone without taking his eyes off the road. "I'm betting it's either Rafe or my father. Would you mind checking?"

She checked her own phone. "Actually, it's my father."

"Ronald? I wonder why he's calling me instead of you?"

Chase's mouth compressed. "Maybe The Barron called him after our meeting."

She grinned at his confusion. "Chase, it's my father on my phone."

"What...?" He spared her a swift, startled glance. "Hell, I swear I've changed that ringtone at least twenty different times. Don't tell me..." His mouth eased into the first smile she'd seen they'd left San Francisco. "Seriously? Again?"

"'Fraid so. We must have some sort of weird telepathy going on."

"I guarantee that's what my mother would believe."

She took the call and chatted with her father for a few minutes. He seemed preoccupied, but that was nothing new. To her surprise, Chase left the freeway a couple of exits early and headed for the coast road. She didn't ask where they were going, preferring to be surprised. Just as she ended her conversation, Chase pulled off the road at Busted Bluff and parked the car.

The night closed in around them. In the distance Emma could hear the sounds of the ocean, the relentless surge of waves against beach. The leaves of a nearby eucalyptus stirred in response to a benevolent breeze. Just past the bluff, a huge orange-tinted moon sank toward the sea, its bottom edge already lapping against the watery horizon.

"Emma... There's something I need to tell you," Chase began.

"Does it have anything to do with Worth Industries now being owned by Cameron Enterprises? Or were you about to tell me the real reason you whisked me off to San Francisco?"

"I whisked you off to San Francisco because my father requested we make a command appearance. But I will admit the timing proved convenient."

She nodded, grateful for the shadows that concealed her expression. "I understand. Everyone worried that I'd kick up a fuss."

"There isn't anything you could have done to stop the sale going through," he informed her. Compassion rippled through his words. "Even so, I didn't see any point in rubbing your nose in it. Even if my father hadn't called, I would have taken you somewhere romantic for the weekend. I'm just sorry the romance part of the trip didn't work out the way we planned. Maybe another weekend."

She turned to study Chase. "You're not like him, you know."

"Sorry?"

She smiled at the icicles clinging to that single word. She also ignored them. "You're not like your father."

"Don't be ridiculous. I learned ruthless at his knee."

She dismissed his comment with a quick shake of her head. "I don't see how that's possible since you rarely saw him, let alone his knee."

"Emma—"

"Do you really think I don't understand?"

"Drop it, sweetheart. There's nothing to understand."

"You went to live with the man at ten, Chase. You were just a child. It isn't difficult to figure out how and why that happened."

He stared out the front windshield, his jaw set in stone. "Okay, fine. Get it off your chest. What did you figure out?"

"Obviously, Karis can't have children and for reasons of his own The Barron won't divorce her. Either she has something on him or he actually loves her. Otherwise he would have married someone else long ago and fathered a brood of legitimate sons to carry on the Barron name."

For a moment, Chase relaxed enough to smile. "There's still that potential. If it happens, he'll disinherit me again."

Emma lifted an eyebrow. "Again?"

"I think I'm hovering near half a dozen times."

"Whenever you say no to him?" she guessed.

"Pretty much."

"I assume that once The Barron discovered that Karis couldn't or wouldn't bear him any legitimate children, he decided to claim you."

Chase shrugged. "Does it matter?"

"Not really, other than it gives a clear indication of his overall character. I was dead serious when I said I know why he never adopted you."

"Why?" he whispered.

"Because he always anticipated, despite Karis, that one day he'd have legitimate children and could simply shunt you to one side in favor of his 'real' sons and daughters. And I know one more thing, too. I can tell you precisely why you left your mother and went with him."

"Don't go there, Emma. Not there." The icicles were back. This time he'd combined them with a hard, cold warning that blazed with caution lights and trip wires. Trip wires that threatened imminent detonation if she dared trespass any further.

She knocked aside the caution lights and yanked on the first wire. "He threatened your mother, didn't he?"

A single, bitterly crude word escaped Chase. He slammed from the car and paced to the edge of the bluff. The moon gilded him in silver, turning his hair almost as pale as Rafe's. She gave him a moment to gather up his self-control and then joined him.

"How did you know?" he asked, keeping his back to her.

"I met both of your parents."

He swung around. With the moon behind him, shadows consumed his face. "And that's all it took?"

"That's all it took," she confirmed. "There's no inducement in the world that would convince a ten-year-old boy to leave a mother as delightful and quirky as Penny for a man as callous and arrogant as Tiberius Barron, especially not once you'd had your first taste of prep school."

"I managed."

"Yes, you did. You protected your mother from your father. And then you worked every hour of every day to make yourself into a man as powerful and wealthy as The Barron so you could continue to protect her, as well as provide her with every material advantage she could ever wish for. You managed all that, and you did it without turning into him. You're not your father's son, Chase, and you never will be."

"How can you be so sure?" The question slipped into the night, filled with angst. It threatened to break her heart. She went to him, wrapped him up in her warmth. Held him tight until the coldness broke and the tension snapped. He buried his face in her hair. "Oh, God, Emma. And they call me a bastard. He wouldn't marry her. Wouldn't dream of marrying her because she wasn't good enough for him."

"It was the other way around, Chase." She slipped her fingers into his dense, crisp hair and forced him to look at her. "Have you ever asked your mother whether she would have married The Barron if he'd asked?"

"No, of course not, because he never would have."

She released a short, impatient laugh. "Sometimes you amaze me, Chase. I suggest you do ask her, although I can tell you her answer."

He stiffened. "Which is?"

"She'd never have married him. Not ever." Slowly, carefully, Emma slid her arms around Chase's neck. "If she'd told you as much, would you still have gone to live with your father?"

He closed his eyes. "Yes."

"Because he threatened to hurt her financially. To take away her home or her job. Or maybe he threatened to take her to court and accuse her of being a bad mother." Chase's flinch gave her the answer. "I am so sorry. You couldn't have suspected he would never have followed through."

"You don't know my father very well if you think that."

"I know my own father. They're somewhat alike, yours and mine. Men as powerful as our fathers, who spend so much of their life in the limelight, would never have risked the adverse publicity. And taking you from your mother, no matter how he tried to slant it, wouldn't have looked good. Plus, he could never have gotten Karis to play the part of the doting stepmother.

not with video cameras recording her every little glance and intonation."

"Why are you telling me all this?"

The moonlight fell full on her face. She didn't doubt that it sliced through all pretense and gave expression to her every thought and emotion and vulnerability. "If we're going to marry, we need to resolve the issues from the past. It's the only way to keep history from repeating itself. You should talk to your mother and explain what happened. Let her know that you didn't abandon her because your father bribed you with promises of toys and trips and spectacular allowances."

"You said… If we're going to marry." His gaze turned razor-sharp. "Don't mess with me, Emma. Not now. This is too important."

She took a deep breath. "I'm willing to move in with you, assuming the offer is still available."

"It's still available. It's definitely still available." He reached into his pocket and pulled out a small, square jewelry box. Thumbing open the lid, he removed the ring inside. "But if we're going to move in together, I'd like you to wear this when we do."

The ring was a spectacular pink diamond that looked close to five karats. She laughed through a sudden mist of tears when she realized he'd chosen a princess cut. He took her hand in his and, beneath the setting moon, slipped the ring on to her finger. It glittered with a magical fire.

"Marry me, Emma," Chase said.

Then he gathered her in his arms and kissed her. There beneath the velvet canopy of the moon and stars, with a timeless surf surging far beneath their feet, Emma faced the truth. She loved this man. More than anything in the world she wanted to be his wife, to bear the child she carried and possibly a few more. To tumble through the years with Chase, creating the sort of enduring relationship that would still be young and fresh and passionate when they were old and gray.

She broke off the kiss with a sigh of utter contentment. "Yes,

Chase. I'll marry you." She snatched one last kiss, one he would have deepened if she hadn't reluctantly pulled back. "Take me home."

"You mean to the condo? That's not home." He inclined his head toward the coast road. "Our home is that way. Or it soon will be. My offer on the house we previewed was accepted. It'll be available by the end of the month."

"That soon?" she asked, stunned.

He swung her into his arms and carried her toward the car. "Sometimes being a tough, ruthless businessman is a good thing."

She rested her head against his shoulder. "Color me shocked, amazed and delighted."

"I think I'd rather color you naked."

She laughed. "That, too."

"So what do you have on tap for today? Any chance we can stay here and hang out at the condo all day?" Chase asked over breakfast the next morning.

"Ana Rodriguez is in town. We're having lunch." Emma waggled the fingers of her left hand in Chase's direction. "I have a lot of news to share."

"Actually, you have more than you know. I forgot to mention something to you last night."

"I'm not surprised. We were a tad busy." He grinned, a feral, wolfish baring of teeth that warned that it wouldn't take much to convince him to try for an encore performance. A slight blush touched her cheeks. It would be well worth repeating, too. They'd both been ravenous. She sucked in a swift breath and fought for control. "So what did you forget to tell me?"

"As a condition of the sale, your father requested that you be named to the board of Hannah's Hope."

It took an instant for the name to register. "Oh, right. Dad told me about the charity Rafe plans to start up. It's in his mother's honor, isn't it?"

"That's right. The charity promotes literacy since it was a cause that Hannah supported during her lifetime."

Emma speared a slice of pineapple. "Tell me the truth, Chase, is Rafe sincere about the charity, or is this just some clever PR move to take the focus off his plans for Worth Industries?"

"First, it's not Worth anymore, but Cameron Enterprises. And second, Rafe is totally sincere about anything and everything connected to his mother. Right now he's looking to hire someone to head the foundation."

That certainly showed Chase's brother in a new, more positive light. "And my position on the board?" she probed. "Will it carry actual weight or am I merely a figurehead?"

"That's up to you. You devote a lot of energy to It's Time. Plus your pregnancy is going to affect your workload. But I guarantee that any spare hours you're willing to donate to Hannah's Hope will be appreciated."

"I'd like that."

Chase laughed. "You sound surprised."

"I guess I am. I never thought Rafe and I would agree on anything. But this sounds like an excellent cause." She speared another section of pineapple and considered it with a frown. "I do have one suggestion, though."

"Which is?"

The suspicion underscoring the question amused her. "I would recommend that in addition to finding someone to head the foundation that he also find a celebrity to act as spokesperson for it."

"That's an excellent suggestion. You know… Rafe and I are good friends with Ward Miller. He might make an excellent spokesperson for the charity."

"Ward Miller, the musician?" she asked, impressed. "How do you know him?"

"We met years ago. I handle some of his investments. I'll suggest Rafe get in touch with him about your idea. And now…" She only had time to swallow the sliver of pineapple before he tipped her out of her chair and into his arms. "I have an excellent suggestion of my own."

She couldn't ever remember laughing as much as she had with Chase over the past few weeks. "And what would that be?"

His mouth hovered close to the side of her face and he whispered the most sinfully delicious proposition into her ear. She fought to draw breath, fought even harder to keep her knees locked in place when they wanted to melt to the floor taking her along for the ride.

"Well, Ms. Worth?" he asked. "What do you think of my suggestion?"

She swallowed. Hard. "I think it's a distinct possibility, Mr. Larson."

"I was hoping you'd say that."

By the time Emma and Chase climbed out of bed several hours later, showered and scrambled into their clothing once again, it was almost time for her lunch date at the Tidal Pool with Ana. The two women arrived at the Vista del Mar Beach and Tennis Club at the exact same moment, and after exchanging enthusiastic hugs, they followed the hostess to a secluded table for two in a corner of the restaurant where they could talk without being overheard.

The minute Ana spotted Emma's engagement ring, her mouth dropped open. "What…? When…? How…?" She shook her head with a laugh. "Actually, the most important question is who?"

Emma chuckled. "His name is Chase Larson. You met him when we ran into each other outside of the Bistro earlier this month."

"Oh, yeah. I remember him." She made an *mmm* sound. "He was hot."

Emma couldn't deny it and didn't bother trying. "He's amazing."

"And what a rock. Is that a pink diamond?"

"Why, yes it is."

"Why, aren't you the lucky one."

Once the laughter died, Emma decided she might as well tell Ana the rest of her news and get it out into the open. "There's something else you should know. In fact, I'm surprised Nilda hasn't mentioned it already."

Ana shoved her menu to one side and waved off the waitress. "Not a word. And trust me, I will have something to say to my mother about that particular oversight."

"I'm pregnant. Closing in on twelve weeks now."

Ana's mouth dropped open again and her gaze lowered automatically to Emma's waistline. "Pregnant. I just... I don't know what to say."

"Congratulations? Best wishes?"

Her friend launched herself from her chair and flew to Emma's side, enveloping her in a tight hug. "Of course, congratulations and best wishes. I'm so pleased for you." She pulled back. "Are you happy? I mean really happy? Oh, don't even bother answering. I can see from your expression that you're head over heels in love with the guy."

Emma smiled tremulously. "I am. I'm crazy about him. And happier than I ever thought possible."

"Then that's all that matters." Ana resumed her seat and leaned forward. "So, when and where is the big wedding. When are you due? What's he like? Come on, Em. Tell me everything."

Emma ticked off on her fingers. "I'm not certain, but it'll be soon. Someplace private, probably on the estate. The baby is due in the middle of August. Perfect." Emma reached across the table and caught Ana's hand in hers. "And promise me you'll be at the wedding no matter what movie set you're working on."

"I do promise since..." Ana blew out a breath. "I'm not sure I'm going back to L.A."

It was Emma's turn to stare in disbelief. "Why not? I thought you loved your job."

"I did at first. But I'm becoming more and more disenchanted."

Emma frowned in concern. "Why? What happened?"

"Let's just say that a certain Hollywood megastar couple aren't as faithful as everyone claims."

"No!"

"Oh, yes." Ana leaned in and lowered her voice. "The husband of said couple, who shall remain forever nameless, but whose costumes I've had the dubious pleasure of designing, has been hitting on me for the past three months. The final straw came when he backed me into a corner this week and thought I'd swoon for joy over his star treatment tonsillectomy."

"Did you slap him?"

"Tempting. Very, very tempting. But if I'd done that I'd have been fired and I can't afford to give up my old job until I have a new one. I swear, if It's Time actually hired help instead of using volunteers, I'd fill out an application here and now. The only thing I love more than costume design is my charity work." She paused long enough to draw breath. "Lord, I'm ranting, aren't I?"

"If anyone deserves to, you do," Emma reassured her.

Ana sighed. "I'll tell you, Em. I've had it with these Hollywood types who hit it big and think it entitles them to take whatever or whomever they want. I swear, I will never trust the rich and famous ever again."

"I don't blame you. I wouldn't, either."

Ana laughed and picked up the menu again. "What do you say we forget all about my problems and just enjoy lunch?"

It wasn't until they were halfway through their meal that a possible solution to Ana's problem occurred to Emma. "You know...Rafe Cameron is starting up a charitable foundation to support literacy."

"Cameron..." Ana's brow wrinkled in thought. "The man who just bought out your dad's business?"

"That's the one. They're looking for someone to run it. It's called Hannah's Hope. You'd be perfect to head the project."

"I don't know, Em." Ana couldn't hide her uncertainty. "It sounds like a wonderful opportunity. But I'm not sure I'm qualified."

Emma refused to let her off the hook so easily. "I know you. I know how much time and energy you put into charitable work. Plus, you have all the ins and outs down cold."

"Why would Rafe Cameron want me? He has no idea what I'm capable of."

"True. But according to Chase, Rafe isn't the one making the final decision. At least, he won't be making it without direction from the board of directors for the charity. And since I sit on the board..." She trailed off with a smile.

"Tell me you're joking."

"Not even a little."

"If there's even the smallest chance they'll consider me, sign me up."

"Consider it done."

The two women chatted for the next hour while they ate their lunch, then parted ways. Pleased with the possibility that Ana might be returning to Vista del Mar, and better yet, running Hannah's Hope, Emma continued on to It's Time. She spent the rest of the afternoon tackling the pile of paperwork that had built up in her absence. Finally ready to call it a day, she decided to drop by the estate and see how her father was holding up now that he'd finalized the sale of Worth Industries to Rafe.

To her surprise, he didn't answer his cell phone and she didn't find him at home. "He's at work," Nilda offered helpfully.

"What's he doing there?"

Ana's mother shrugged. "He had a call from Señor Cameron a few hours ago and went in."

"That didn't take long. I would have thought Rafe capable of running the business for more than a few days without needing Dad to come rushing to the rescue."

Emma decided to go ahead and drive over to the corporate campus and see what was going on. If she didn't find her father there, she'd get up with him in the morning. She yawned, exhaustion setting in. More and more she found it difficult to continue at the same pace she had in the past. She hated the idea of cutting back on her workload at the shelter, but the health of the baby was paramount and she wouldn't do anything to jeopardize that.

She pulled into the campus parking lot, surprised to see a massive jam of cars and trucks. Some were news vans with huge dish antennas on top and their call letters and station channels emblazoned on all sides. What in the world was going on? She scooted into the first available space. After locking the car, she wandered closer to the crowd. They were gathered outside the front of the main office building, a multistory glass-and-steel structure surrounded by a neatly trimmed grassy expanse, landscaped shrubs and tidy garden areas.

As she approached she saw they'd set up a platform with chairs and a podium. Rafe stood behind the microphone, sunlight glistening off his pale blond hair. His deep voice bounced off the glass behind him and echoed across the crowd. She couldn't make out the exact words, but she saw her father standing behind him in the shadows of the building, nodding in apparent agreement.

To her surprise, the instant Chase caught sight of her, he detached himself from those on the platform and vaulted to the ground. His long strides ate up the distance between them and when he reached her, he wrapped an arm around her and dropped a swift, yet delightfully thorough kiss on her mouth.

"I'm glad you made it," he said in greeting.

"It's purely by chance. I had no idea there was any sort of ceremony planned," she answered truthfully. "What's going on?"

"I assumed your father would have told you."

She shook her head, then froze. Rafe made a sweeping gesture and behind him a large tarp dropped to the ground. Where once a sign proudly declared Worth Industries, now it read Cameron Enterprises. For some reason it struck her like an unexpected blow to the heart.

* * *

Chase watched the tarp drift to the ground and heard the slight gasp of pain Emma couldn't quite control. He shot her a sharp look, caught the devastation in her expression and instantly swung her in a swift half circle. "Let's go."

"No, it's all right," she insisted. "I'm fine."

"I can see it's not all right and that you're not fine. Now I understand why your father didn't mention the ceremony to you." He scanned the parking lot. "Where's your car?"

She pointed. "Seriously, Chase. It just caught me off guard. There's no reason you can't rejoin them on the podium. I'll see you at the condo once you're through here."

"You'll see me right now because I intend to be in your rearview mirror every inch of the way between here and my condo."

She must have realized the futility of further argument. With a brisk nod, she crossed the parking lot to her car. As promised, he kept behind her the entire way, careful not to crowd her, but keeping her in sight nonetheless.

"You all right?" he asked the minute they walked through the front door.

"For the last time, I'm fine. The change in name just took me by surprise, that's all." She attempted a smile, one that didn't fool him for a minute. "Silly, really. You even mentioned this morning that it wasn't Worth Industries anymore, but Cameron Enterprises. I guess it didn't sink in until I saw the sign."

"And it hit you."

Her mouth trembled for a split second before she brought it under tight control. "Like a ton of bricks," she reluctantly admitted. "Even though I've never been interested in running the business, I don't think I realized that it was such an integral part of me. Of my identity."

"Come here." She didn't hesitate, but went into his arms. He wrapped her up tight. "It's all going to work out, you'll see."

"I know it will."

"Are you hungry? I can whip something up. Actually, I make the best takeout you ever tasted."

That won him a smile. After a short debate, he placed a call to one of Emma's favorite Mexican restaurants. Within the hour, they were curled up together on a lounger on the deck, sharing each other's choices. Once through, they watched while day transitioned into evening, the sun drowning itself in the ocean, its fierce light no match for the chilly ocean depths that seemed to consume it bite by bite. It wasn't until a crisp wind swept off the water that Emma shifted within Chase's embrace.

"Take me to bed," she whispered. "I need you. I need to be in your arms. I need you to make love to me."

"You read my mind."

The two drifted in the direction of the bedroom, their progress stuttering to a halt whenever they lost themselves in the kisses they couldn't quite bring themselves to postpone. Darkness had invaded the bedroom by the time they reached it, gathering in deep, quiet shadows. Just enough ambient light slipped into the room for Chase to find the buttons of Emma's jacket, the zip of her skirt, to lift her silk shell up and off. The bits and pieces of her clothing drifted away, faint pools of pale color against the thick, plush carpeting. He traced the outline of her bra and her breath hitched.

Their phones rang almost simultaneously and he swore in annoyance. They broke apart long enough to fumble for them. "Dad," Emma said, pulling her phone from her jacket pocket.

He retrieved his from his trousers. "Rafe. Let them go to voice mail. We can deal with whatever it is in the morning." He tossed his BlackBerry onto the nightstand table, took hers and tossed it alongside. "Now, where were we?"

He found her mouth again and she opened to him. His tongue dipped inward and he tasted her with a blatant hunger that skated the edge of passion. Her lip beckoned and he caught it between his teeth and tugged. "I've been fantasizing about that lip all day." He soothed it with a kiss. "It's been taunting me. Plump, saucy little lip."

Her laugh turned to a moan when he deepened the kiss once more and she brushed against him with teasing, restless movements. Her hands fluttered, landed, then pushed and shoved until she'd stripped away his shirt, before returning to settle on his bare chest. Her nails scraped across the taut planes, raking his nipples. It plunged him into mindless need.

Off. Bed. In. The words were a mindless chant in his head. Clothes off. Fall onto bed. In, in, in. Driving and plunging and drenching himself in her. How was it possible that he possessed so little control when he was a man renowned for his control? It had only been this way with Emma, never with any other woman. He didn't understand it, had never understood it. Not that it changed a damn thing.

Her bra fell first beneath his onslaught and he took the time to fill his hands with her sensitive breasts, to worship them with tongue and teeth. To taste their burgeoning sweetness until she quivered against him, her breath coming in helpless little gasps.

He hadn't managed to get all their clothing off, but he didn't care. Another directive was already crashing down on him, compelling him to act. Bed. Get onto the bed. He eased her backward, falling into a shimmering slice of heaven. In one swift motion he ripped her pantyhose from her legs and shredded her thong. And then he cupped her. Her sweet, delicate scent drove him insane, as did the burning heat of her.

In. In. In. He knew that's what came next, but for the life of him he couldn't seem to get past the softness of her or the generous give of her body or the heady impact she had on every last one of his five senses. He just wanted to wallow in the moment, lapping it up in great greedy gulps. Maybe he would have if she hadn't taken the initiative away from him by unzipping his trousers and freeing him.

She filled her hands with him, the coolness against his overheated flesh nearly unmanning him. She shaped him. Stroked. Squeezed until his brain almost exploded. But it was her sigh that was the final straw. It was the sort of sigh women made when they bit into a particularly delectable sliver of chocolate. The sort of sigh they made when they closed their eyes and rolled it across their tongue, savoring the sweet explosion of flavor. The sort of sigh that made women think of rich, dark Godiva and men think of rich, dark sex.

That sigh did him in.

He lifted her, parted her, surged toward salvation, sheathing himself in one swift motion. Her cry of encouragement compelled him, drove him to take her harder and faster, no matter how much he might want to slow the moment. Savor it. He tried to build gradually toward the glittering peak, but the enormity of it all crashed over him like a wave driven before a gale.

He slammed into his climax, sweeping her along with him, shaken to the very core, drained dry in one immense release. He gave her everything he had, heart and mind, body and soul. And it was in that moment of complete and utter clarity—a moment stripped of all artifice and control, a moment that left him more vulnerable than he could ever remember—that he faced the incontrovertible truth.

He loved Emma. He worshipped her. She was his everything and always would be. No matter what it took, he'd prove that to her. Bind her and protect her, encourage and support her. And he'd love her beyond reason until the end of his days. He started to tell her, to confess how deeply he cared. But by the time the power of speech returned, Emma was sound asleep.

A faint *ping* awoke Emma the next morning, along with an irritating vibration. She lifted her head and glared in the direction of the nightstand table. Someone had sent an email message to her BlackBerry.

She groped for the phone and accessed the message with a yawn, struggling to make sense of it. She stared blurry-eyed at the words for an endless moment before the scramble of letters rearranged itself into cogent sentences.

Chase, thanks for distracting Emma these past few weeks. Or should I say thanks for seducing her into compliance? She can't cause me any further problems now. Consider your job officially done. When do you return to NY? Rafe

Ten

It took several long seconds for the message to sink in.

The instant it did, Emma exploded from the bed. All this time. All this time she believed Chase actually cared for her, that he was falling in love with her. That even if there'd been no baby, something existed between them that promised a future together.

But with one simple message all her foolish dreams shattered, scattering around her like shards of glass, ready to cut and stab the unwary. Tears burned her eyes. She'd certainly been unwary, hadn't she? Instead of finding something lasting, something enduring, she'd placed her trust in the most fragile of commodities. A man who put finances ahead of every other consideration. A man like her father.

She'd trusted Chase, someone who made his living playing the odds. This time he'd played the odds with her and almost pulled it off. He would have pulled it off, if she hadn't gotten that email.

He didn't love her. Couldn't love her. He simply wanted to

nsure that his child didn't come into the world a bastard. All his time she'd believed he was nothing like The Barron. And ll this time, Chase had been a perfectly replicated chip off the ld Barron block. She'd witnessed her own mother's devastation when Ronald Worth had been unable to love her the way she raved. How it had destroyed her. Marriage to Chase would uarantee that history repeated itself.

Emma yanked out the spare clothes she kept stashed in the loset of the master bedroom. How could she have been so polish? Chase had been upfront about his plan to marry her or the sake of their child. He'd even suggested a temporary narriage. Whatever it took so long as their baby came into the world bearing his name. When that hadn't worked, he'd used any nd all means within his power—including seducing her—to chieve his ends. She dressed in quick, jerky movements, truggling to see through eyes gone blind with tears.

Even better, his grand seduction had kept her distracted y emotion at a time she should have focused her energy on rotecting the employees of Worth Industries. Not Worth ndustries, not anymore. Cameron Enterprises. Rafe's employees vould be the ones to suffer now if he decided to strip Worth are.

Emma fought to button her jeans, dismayed to discover they vouldn't close anymore. It was the last straw. Tears flowed reely. She heard the rush of pounding water coming from ne bathroom. She wouldn't get a better opportunity to escape nan while Chase showered. She glanced down at herself and roaned. She didn't doubt for a moment that she looked like madwoman. Her hair was a mess, the buttons of her blouse vere in all the wrong holes, her jeans gaped and not a scrap of nakeup concealed the hollow, bruised expression edging her ace.

Once upon a time, she'd have been conscious of representing Vorth Industries whenever she stepped out the front door. tearful laugh broke free. Only it wasn't Worth Industries

anymore, she reminded herself yet again. She'd stood righ
outside the beautifully landscaped corporate campus whil
Rafe lifted his arm, and with a snap of his fingers, change
Worth Industries into Cameron Enterprises. Now she didn'
have anyone to represent but herself.

The shower shut off, warning that if she planned to avoi
a confrontation with Chase, she'd better leave soon. The tw
BlackBerrys sat side by side on the nightstand table and sh
approached, examining each to determine which was whose
She scanned the incriminating email on Rafe's one final tim
and started to hit the "Mark Unopened" option. Her thum
hovered over the button.

Why bother? she finally decided. Let him see she'd read it
Let him know she'd uncovered his scheme. She tossed Chase'
BlackBerry onto his pillow, the message glowing up at her wit
malicious glee. Then she stripped off her engagement ring an
put it alongside the phone. Snatching up her purse, she swep
from the bedroom and straight out the front door.

Chase entered the bedroom, a towel knotted at his waist
another slung around his neck. "Emma?"

The only reply to his call was the sound of the fron
door slamming closed. He scanned the room in a swift, all
encompassing glance. Emma's clothing no longer decorate
the floor. The closet door gaped and the spare outfit she kep
stored there was gone. Her purse was also missing. His gaz
landed on the bed and the diamond ring that glittered alongsid
his BlackBerry. He snatched up both, read Rafe's email an
swore viciously.

It didn't take any of his finely tuned analytical skills to gues
what had happened. He reached the front door in five second
flat and jerked it open. Emma was just backing out of the spac
where she'd parked her car the night before. He planted himsel
squarely in her path. Her brakes squealed and the car bumpe
bounced to a stop inches from his kneecaps.

He circled the car to her driver's-side door and made a circular, rolling-down motion. She lowered the tinted window, her expression one of undisguised fury. But it was the tears sliding down her cheeks that hit him like a fist to the gut. "It's not what you think," he informed her.

"Don't hand me that, Chase. It's exactly what I think. Rafe's been calling the shots from the minute we met. For all I know he arranged for our accidental meeting back in November so you could gather intel on the Worths even then." She wrapped annoying little air quotes around the words *accidental meeting*.

"Damn it, Emma, that's not true and you know it." He shot a hand through his damp hair. "Be reasonable. Come back inside and let's discuss the situation in a rational manner like two civilized adults. I'm practically naked here, honey."

She shook her head before he even finished speaking. "As far as I'm concerned there's nothing left to discuss."

Son of a bitch! "I'm not going to stand out here in a towel arguing with you."

"I didn't ask you to." She threw the car in Reverse and pulled out of the parking spot. "Let it go, Chase. You and Rafe both got what you wanted. Be satisfied with that."

"You're pregnant with my child, Emma. That hasn't changed."

"No, it hasn't, but I'll tell you what." She smiled brightly, a difficult proposition considering the tears overflowing her eyes. "I'll get you the number of our family lawyer and you can funnel all of your concerns and requests through him."

She didn't give him time to offer any further arguments. She hit a button and her window silently rose, hiding her from view. Before he could think of a way to stop her, she pulled down the drive, through the gate and onto the main road. Turning, Chase shot back into the condo. He threw on jeans, snagged a shirt and shoved his feet into a pair of loafers. Finally, he snatched up his wallet, BlackBerry—damn Rafe to hell—her engagement ring and his car keys. The entire process took a precious four minutes. Four minutes during which Emma was screaming down the road away from him.

Slamming out of the condo, he hopped into the Fiorano and started the engine with a muted roar. Then he went after her. It didn't matter what it took. It didn't matter what he had to say or promise. Nothing mattered more to him than Emma. His hands clenched around the steering wheel.

Dear God, how he loved her.

Chase shook his head in disbelief. He'd always been so careful, so guarded. Emotions were dangerous. Once people knew which buttons to push, they could get to you and twist you to their agenda. They could hurt you. He'd learned his lesson well at the great age of ten. He'd learned to hide behind a carefully constructed facade. To bury his emotions deep where no one would find them or touch them or wound what mattered most to him. But with Emma...

She'd found a way beneath his guard. Maybe it was because they were both wounded. Maybe because one wary, battered soul recognized another. She'd been hurt, too, and had learned to guard herself just as he had. But from the moment they'd first touched, that had changed. The trappings had melted away, leaving a core of honesty between them.

Chase's mouth tightened. Or it had until Rafe screwed things up. Until Rafe destroyed that fragile, delicate connection, tainting it with doubt and suspicion. He pulled off the highway at the exit Emma would have taken to return to the Worth estate. He wanted to get to her before she had the opportunity to barricade herself behind thick walls and locked doors. Before Ronald could step between them and interfere. To explain to her how it had all gone down and let her see the truth in his eyes and hear it in his voice. To confess what he should have last night.

To tell her he loved her.

Traffic grew heavier and the lights turned against him, but

he managed to dart and weave his way forward until he caught a glimpse of a distinctive white BMW. Okay, if he squeezed around a couple more cars and hit one of the next few lights just right—an iffy proposition, he was forced to admit—he'd have her. He didn't want to get too close. He wasn't racing her, merely pacing the drive so he'd pull into the Worth estate right on her bumper.

At the next intersection, she turned right and a hard, grim smile ripped across his mouth. Perfect. He'd have her within the next block. He made the turn and saw Emma sitting at a red light. She was the first in line and there were several cars stacked between them. With luck she wouldn't notice him, though with a screaming red Ferrari, it was a bit tough to fade into the background. Black, he reminded himself. Next time he'd rent a black car. You just couldn't go wrong with basic black. The light turned green and Emma pulled into the intersection.

And that's when it happened.

One minute life proceeded along normal, if turbulent channels, and the next it was unalterably changed, never to be the same again. A pickup came shooting through the light at a right angle to Emma's BMW. It was the oddest sensation. Everything slowed, like a recording put on pause and then allowed to creep forward frame by hideous frame. It seemed as though someone had pushed the mute button on the sound, as well, though for years afterward the screech of brakes and shriek of metal would wrench Chase from a dead sleep, shouting out a futile warning.

Pure raw sunshine shot down from the heavens, spotlighting the intersection. He opened his mouth, thought he roared out a single word…"No!" But he couldn't be certain. Maybe he called Emma's name. Maybe both. The black pickup, all tricked out with flames painted on the side and chrome everything, careened along its path of doom. It had been jacked up off the ground with special suspension and huge off-road tires that chewed up deserts and blasted through mud. This time it blasted through Emma.

Her dainty cabriolet never stood a chance. The truck T-boned the smaller vehicle, sending it careening like a Ping-Pong ball, slamming first into the post of a streetlight and then into a helpless car sitting at the same red light the pickup had run. The BMW came to a rest, unrecognizable as the car it had once been, smoke and steam pouring from the crumbled bits and pieces that remained.

For a brief instant everything froze, a frightening tableau that defied understanding and belief. Then all hell broke loose. Around him people scrambled for their cells. Others ran toward the scene of the crash. The driver of the pickup stumbled out of the cab and dropped to the pavement on his hands and knees. No movement came from the BMW.

Every ounce of athletic grace and ability deserted Chase in those precious moments after the accident. He fumbled for the door and couldn't seem to figure out how to operate the handle. When he finally got it opened, he tripped, losing one of his shoes. He kicked off the other and ran barefoot toward the scene of the accident. Bare-chested, too, since he'd never gotten around to shrugging on his shirt. Not that he cared. In that moment, nothing mattered but Emma. He dodged open car doors and milling witnesses, evading the hands that reached for him, ignoring the incomprehensible words tossed his way.

By the time Chase reached the intersection, the police were on the scene. He didn't understand where they'd come from or how they'd arrived so quickly. He could only thank God they had. Right until one of the officers stopped him from getting to Emma.

The policeman straight-armed him, holding him at bay. "Please stay back, sir."

"No!" He knocked the officer's arm away. "You don't understand. I have to get to Emma—"

The arm came up again, this time fisting around his biceps.

Sunlight bounced off the gold name tag he wore. Garcia. Officer Garcia. Of course. It would be. "I said, stand back. There's an injured woman. We need to keep the area clear for emergency personnel."

"She's mine. That woman is mine. It's Emma. Emma Worth."

Garcia's eyes widened. "The Worth heiress? Ronald Worth's daughter?"

"Yes." Chase attempted to shove past the officer again. "Let me through. She's my fiancée. I have to get to her."

Sympathy gleamed in the cop's eyes. "I'm sorry, I can't let you do that. There's a doctor with her now. He was in the vehicle behind hers."

Chase fought to breathe. "Is she…?" He sucked air into his lungs, unable to use the *d* word, but Garcia understood.

"No, no. She's alive. But you have to let them work on her."

"She's pregnant." He strained to move past the policeman. "She's pregnant with my baby."

"We'll let the doctor know. We'll also let him know you're here." Compassion rippled across Garcia's expression and colored his voice. "As soon as he okays it, I'll let you through, I promise."

"I need to be with her."

"Trust me, I understand."

The next five minutes felt like an eternity, filled with fear and helplessness. In the distance Chase heard a siren gradually, oh, so gradually, approaching. It seemed to be moving in slow motion like everything else around him. At long last one of the policemen stationed beside the remains of Emma's car waved in Garcia's direction.

"Go ahead," the officer instructed.

Chase raced barefoot through the shards of metal and broken glass, avoiding most of it, ignoring what he didn't manage to avoid. He crouched beside the driver's door. Emma still sat trapped inside the crushed metal, her eyes closed. A powdery residue clung to everything. That didn't worry him since he could tell it came from the exploded air bags that surrounded her. The blood, on the other hand, scared the hell out of him.

"She's pregnant," Chase informed the man he identified as the doctor.

"So I understand."

"Is she going to be all right?"

"She's been in and out of consciousness. We'll have a better idea once we get her to the hospital and run some tests."

"Is she—" His voice broke and he couldn't continue. Couldn't say the words. He wasn't even sure he could handle the answer.

The doctor rested a hand on Chase's shoulder. "She's going to live. Thank God for air bags and well-built automobiles."

Relief charged through him, bringing tears to his eyes. But his relief was short-lived. "And our baby?"

"I'm sorry." Pity. His pity gave Chase the untenable answer. "I can't answer that."

Something strange had occurred.

Emma struggled to wrap her mind around it but found she couldn't. The ability to focus eluded her. Voices came and went, phasing in and out. She could hear the concern sweeping beneath the words, but each time she attempted to latch onto one of the comments, it drifted just out of range.

Darkness beckoned and for a short time she succumbed to its allure, but something—no, someone—kept pulling her back, forcing her into that world of pain and confusion. The voice came again, coaxing and pleading. She tried to open her eyes in response but harsh light radiated from behind her closed eyelids, stabbing into her head. Opening her eyes would allow the pain in and she'd do just about anything to prevent that from happening.

"Don't want to," she attempted to explain.

"Don't want to...what, sweetheart?"

Oh. She knew that voice. It was Chase's voice. Her brows tugged together. Something about Chase. Something that caused even more pain. Only this wasn't a physical hurt, but an emotional one.

"Emma, what don't you want?"

The question compelled her to answer, brooked no opposition. "Don't want to open my eyes. Hurts."

"That's okay." For some reason her complaint pleased him. Relief rippled through the simple words. "You can keep them closed."

"What happened?" Because clearly, something had. Something bad. Something that urged her to step back into the blackness that offered peace and an avenue of escape.

"You were in a car accident, Emma."

It took a moment to process the words. Some part of her was screaming, begging her to drift away for a while and not analyze the information. Thinking about it, looking too closely, wouldn't just bring more pain, but agony. And then it hit her.

"The baby?"

"We don't know, Emma." But she could hear the answer in his voice. A bitter coldness swept through her, intensifying the hurt to unbearable levels. Helpless tears slid down her face. "They're about to take you to the hospital. Hang in there, sweetheart."

The darkness beckoned again and this time she didn't hesitate. She threw herself into its embrace.

"How is she?"

Chase looked up from where he'd been sitting slumped, staring at his heavily bandaged feet, to find Rafe approaching at a swift clip. How his brother had found him in the warren of hospital hallways, Chase had no idea. Right now, he waited outside of the room they'd assigned Emma while the umpteenth doctor performed the umpteenth examination on her.

"She lost our baby, Rafe. That's how she is." His hands clenched into fists. "They haven't told me, yet, but I overheard her doctors talking. They were discussing her miscarriage. They're in with her now."

"I'm sorry, Chase."

He heard his brother's words, processed them on some gut level. But instead of finding solace in them, that simple apology filled him with fury. Over the past two-plus decades he'd learned to stuff that anger into a deep, dark hole. To interact with the world from a calm, unemotional distance. In the split second it took Chase to absorb his brother's words, that calm vanished. For good. The hole split open and all the hurt, all the misery, all the suffering he'd experienced over the years he'd been known as Barron's Bastard came rushing to the surface.

"Sorry," Chase repeated softly. He came off his chair and caught Rafe by his elegantly knotted tie and slammed him into the wall. Pain ripped through his feet, which only drove his wrath to greater heights. "You're sorry? Do you have any idea why Emma was at that intersection at that particular moment, you son of a bitch?"

"Let go of me, Chase."

"She was there because of you. She was there because she saw that email you sent to my BlackBerry."

Rafe's expression darkened in outrage. "What the hell was she doing reading private emails on your BlackBerry? Damn it, Larson. It's not my fault that she went behind your back and checked up on you."

"It is your fault. It's all your fault." Grief howled through him. "Why do you think I'm with her, Rafe? Have you ever wondered?"

A wintry remoteness swept across Rafe's demeanor and settled into his eyes and attitude. "Because I asked you to keep an eye on her. To distract her while I sewed up the Worth deal. Because doing so lined both of our pockets."

"Not even close."

"Well… And the baby."

"Wrong again. There's only one reason I'm with Emma."

That gave Rafe pause. "I don't get it."

"No, you sure as hell don't. You never have. You've spent so much of your life intent on revenge, filled with rage, that it doesn't even occur to you that I'm with Emma because I love her. I love her more than I thought it possible to love another person." Chase shoved Rafe away with a sound of disgust. "You know what? I'm done."

Rafe eyed him warily. "What do you mean, you're done?"

"It means that whatever you plan to do with Worth Industries—"

"Cameron Enterprises."

Chase slashed the air between them with his hand. "Fine. Cameron Enterprises. Whatever your future plans for the factory, it's all on you. Tear it down brick by brick if that's what you intend, but I want no part of it. I've shown you how the business can be turned around. How you can upgrade the technology and make it even bigger and more viable than ever before. But you don't want to hear any of that, do you?"

"Not particularly."

"Well, you better hear this." He glared at his brother though red-rimmed eyes. "Emma is mine. And I'll do whatever necessary to protect her, even if it means taking you down."

A noise came from behind them. "Um, Chase…?"

Rafe stepped closer, a glacial warning sweeping like a bitter wind across his expression. "You can try and take me down, but it'll never happen."

"Get out of here, Rafe. You've done enough damage." Chase dug the heels of his palms into eyes that burned with misery and exhaustion. "In a few minutes I have to walk into Emma's room and tell her that our baby died. And then I have to hope like hell I can convince her I love her and want to spend the rest of my life with her. Not because of our baby, but because she's the only woman in the world for me."

"Chase."

His name finally penetrated and he spun around. Emma stood in the doorway of her room, garbed in a blue patterned gown. A purple plaster cast encircled her wrist and a sling held her arm close to her side. Her hair was a disaster, the ice-blond strands sticking up at odd angles. Not a lick of makeup touched the porcelain whiteness of her face, a whiteness relieved by a deep violet bruise decorating her cheekbone. In addition her left eye was swollen almost shut and he could tell from personal experience that in a few more hours it would turn black as ebony.

He'd never seen a more beautiful sight in all his life.

"Emma?" He locked his knees in place so the linoleum wouldn't have to catch them on his way down. Then he frowned. "What the hell are you doing out of bed? You should be resting."

"How am I supposed to rest with all the shouting?" Her gaze swept over his shoulder toward where Rafe continued to stand. "Thanks for stopping by. I'll take it from here."

"I'm sorry, Emma," Rafe said. "It was never my intention that you read that message to Chase. I meant it as a joke, but I realize now it was in very poor taste. Worse, it led to your being injured—and the baby…" His throat convulsed and it took him a moment to continue. "I can't tell you how sorry I am for that." For the first time ever, Chase caught a strong note of regret in his brother's voice.

Emma nodded. "I know. It'll be okay. Chase will give you a call in a little while."

Chase stiffened. "Don't tell him that it'll be okay. It won't be okay."

She sagged against the door frame and lifted a hand to her temple. "I'm feeling a little light-headed. I think I should be in bed."

Chase reached her side in two pain-filled swift strides. He'd never felt more helpless in his life. Gently, tenderly, as though she were made of spun glass, he lifted Emma into his arms and limped to the bed. He set her down on the crisp, white sheets. And then, unable to help himself, he crawled in beside her and cautiously pulled her close.

"Are you all right? Am I hurting you?"

"You're not hurting me. And you're not hurting the baby, either."

The words came like a blow to the solar plexus and all the air escaped his lungs in a painful rush. For a split second he couldn't breathe. Couldn't think. She didn't know. Dear God, she didn't know. Why the hell hadn't the doctors told her? "Emma, about the baby..."

"Did you mean what you said to Rafe in the hallway?"

He struggled to shift gears. "What part?"

"Any of it. All of it." She sighed. "But especially the part where you said that you loved me just for me. That you weren't trying to seduce me in order to distract me the way Rafe suggested in his email."

He closed his eyes and pressed a kiss into the halo of tangles on top of her head, careful to avoid the scrapes and bruises. "I meant it. I love you, Emma. It might have taken me a while to figure out that's what I was feeling, but I got there eventually."

"You hid it pretty well."

"I had to."

"Because of your father. So I couldn't use those feelings against you the way he did when you were ten."

"Yes," Chase admitted gruffly.

She tilted her head back and met his gaze. The compassion he read there nearly gutted him. "You're safe with me, you know."

"Am I?"

She cautiously turned so they faced each other. "I love you, Chase. I think I first fell in love with you on a cool November day when we fought over which of us had dibs on a taxi." She opened to him, allowed him to see every thought and feeling. She held nothing back, but gave it all to him. "And I fell in love with you all over again when you sat on the bathroom floor beside me and dumped a dozen pregnancy tests in my lap. You were so gentle and caring and considerate."

A gruff laugh escaped, catching him by surprise. "Please. I'm begging you. Don't tell anyone that. I'm supposed to be a hotshot badass."

A smile flirted with her mouth, then seized hold, growing with each passing second. "Okay. It'll be our secret."

He couldn't believe they were lying here laughing. Nor would they for much longer once Emma knew the truth. "Sweetheart, there's something I have to explain—"

She covered his mouth with the fingers of her good hand. "Not yet. Let's do this first. Do you mind?"

The pain was so great he couldn't speak around it. He simply shook his head.

"I don't care about Worth Industries. I do care about the people and what Rafe's plans might do to them." She continued to hold him with her gaze. "He's going to gut the business, isn't he?"

"Maybe." Chase blew out a sigh. "Probably. I don't think even Rafe knows at this point."

"Then there's still time to change his mind?"

"I hope so." He cupped her chin and tilted it upward. "I'll work on him, I promise."

"Thank you."

He thrust his hand in his pocket and pulled out the ring she'd left behind when she'd left the condo. It seemed ages ago. An eternity ago. "Emma, I love you and I want to marry you. Someday—" He swallowed hard. "Someday I'd like to have children with you. But what matters most is that whatever life throws at us, we deal with it together."

She held out her hand and wiggled her fingers at him. "I

think I'd like to have that ring back on my finger, if you don't mind."

He leaned in and kissed her with cautious passion. At the same time, he slipped the engagement ring onto her hand. He took his time with the kiss, putting every ounce of love and adoration into it that he possessed. And she returned it with the openness and generosity he'd learned was such an innate part of her character.

For a brief moment he thought of their child. He'd have liked to have had a daughter, one as delicate and elegant as her mother. And maybe someday they would. Not in August. But if Emma was willing, soon.

The kiss deepened and the dream faded to the background, replaced by the here and now. He held Emma in his arms…she was safe and sound, and secure. She loved him, as evidenced by the blistering passion lurking in the depths of their kiss. At the earliest possible moment, he intended to make her his wife. Reluctantly, he pulled back.

"I know you've been avoiding this conversation," he began.

Emma stroked his cheek with her good hand. "I didn't lose our baby, Chase."

He closed his eyes. This was going to be far worse than he thought. "Emma—"

"Listen to me, Chase. Look at me." She waited until he did. "The doctors you overheard discussing a miscarriage? I don't know who they were talking about, but it wasn't me. Since this is the prenatal section of the hospital, it could have been any number of women."

He locked his jaw in place as he struggled to accept her words. "You…you didn't lose the baby?"

"I didn't lose the baby," she repeated and smiled. Her smile was the most beautiful thing he'd ever seen. "She's fine. But they want to observe me for the next twenty-four hours to make sure it stays that way."

Chase opened his mouth to ask another question, but something Emma said finally registered. "She?"

"Well, it's still a bit early to be certain, but the sonologist sounded fairly confident. Something about parallel lines being a girl and a dome being a boy. We have lines. Lots of lines." She rested her head on his shoulder and wrapped her good arm around his waist, snuggling against him. "So do you want to discuss names first or should we talk about wedding dates?"

"Uh—"

"Names it is. I'm thinking Penelope after your mother. We could call her Nell for short."

Chase shook his head, dazed. "Nell?"

"Excellent suggestion."

"Emma?"

"Yes, sweetheart?"

"How do you feel about getting married in a hospital gown?"

"I don't care what I'm wearing or where we marry." She stole another kiss. "So long as it's to you."

"I love you, Emma. And I swear to you we'll make sure that our future will have nothing to do with what we experienced in the past. We'll change it for the better. You'll see."

"Of course we will. Because you're not your father and I'm not my mother. We'll make better choices."

She'd given him the perfect answer. For the first time that day he allowed himself to fully relax. To embrace the sense of peace and joy and calm certainty that filled him. Finally, finally, finally he had everything he wanted in his life. Emma, the woman he loved, held safe and secure within his arms. Their precious daughter, still nestled safe within her mother's womb. And in a matter of days, a home. A real home.

A home in which to live out their dreams for a better tomorrow.

* * * * *

Want to get at the root of Rafe Cameron's desire for revenge against the Worths? Turn the page for an exclusive short story by USA TODAY *bestselling author Catherine Mann. And don't miss the next installment of* THE TAKEOVER *miniseries,* SEDUCED: THE UNEXPECTED VIRGIN, *by Emily McKay, available soon from Silhouette Books.*

Fourteen years ago

A newbie waitress at the Vista del Mar Beach and Tennis Club, Sarah Richards still knew the number one rule for servers: Never spill hot coffee on a customer's lap.

But after less than a week at her new after-school job, she almost messed up. Big-time.

Sarah grabbed the hot glass pot with both hands to keep from upending it into onto the middle-aged guy waiting for java to go with his tiramisu. Her nerves, however, were tougher to steady as she stared through the wall-long window.

Where *he* leaned against the hood of his El Camino by the ocean. Rafe Cameron.

The pot searing her hands was almost as hot as the guy outside. Light from the big fat moon overhead glistened on his shaggy blond hair, which brushed the collar of his black T-shirt. Muscles stretched the cotton fabric. He was lean but toned from working construction after school and on weekends. No matter how many times Grandma Kat told her eighteen wasn't grown-up yet, she saw how Rafe was already a man, mature beyond his years from having experienced a lifetime of hurt.

What was he doing outside? And how long would he be there?

A cleared throat brought her attention back into the fancy dining area with lit candles, clanking silver and, most importantly, big-tipping, wealthy patrons she couldn't afford to ignore.

"Sorry about that, Mr. Worth," she said, pouring his coffee, a good idea anyhow before she scalded her hands. "Is there anything else I can get for either of you?"

Ronald Worth was the big kahuna of Vista del Mar. His factory, Worth Industries, employed almost everybody in the town, including her parents and her grandmother. He was pretty much a hard-nosed boss from what she heard. But it was tough not to feel sorry for him right now as he sat having dinner with his little girl, all alone since his wife had died just over a year ago from a sleeping pill overdose.

Nobody knew if it was suicide or an accident, but there were lots of theories out there to pick from. And yeah, people were talking. Vista del Mar was such a tiny town, secrets were tough to keep.

She leaned down toward little Emma Worth, who couldn't be more than about ten or eleven. "Could I get you something else, sweetie? Maybe another scoop of ice cream since this one has pretty much melted all over your brownie."

Emma shook her head without raising her eyes. "No thank you."

Poor kid. The girl might have a reputation as Daddy's spoiled princess, but Sarah wouldn't trade places with her for even a second. She had her family—and maybe soon she would have the attention of the guy she'd just about given up hope would ever notice her.

Suddenly, she panicked. What if he left before she could get out there?

She straightened quickly. "If that's all then, Mr. Worth, I'll send someone over with your check."

Backing away, she almost stumbled over a busboy clearing a table.

"Sorry, Quentin," she apologized quickly before racing to find the manager in the break room so she could claim a seriously bad stomach flu.

Sure she was probably being silly rushing out to meet Rafe this way. He hardly seemed to know she existed even though they'd gone to school together all their lives. She could make a big fool out of herself here. But ohmigod, she would lay awake all night regretting it if she didn't at least take a chance. Before she knew it, their senior year would be over and what if she never had the chance to find out if her crush was real?

Leaving early tonight cost her a promise to pull a Saturday morning breakfast stint—the kiss of death for tips—but it would be totally worth it if she finally, finally got Rafe Cameron to acknowledge she was alive.

She whipped off her apron and stuffed it into her backpack. Making tracks through the steamy kitchen smelling of boiled shrimp, she tucked her shirt in tighter, smoothed a hand over her black pants and chewed her lips to pinken them up. Too bad there wasn't time to change into something other than her standard work uniform of a white shirt and black pants, but, well, she would make up for that at school on Monday by wearing her favorite denim miniskirt.

She pushed out through the back exit.

The cool Pacific wind hit her square in her flushed face. She tasted the salt air mixed with freedom on a crisp January breeze. She hadn't been outside all day except to change classes, then had come straight to work. Sometimes she felt like her life was spent staring through windows at her awesome California beach town. She couldn't remember the last time she'd felt the sand between her toes.

Tonight, that would change.

Shrugging into her sweater, Sarah jogged through the packed lot to where she'd seen Rafe parked on a bluff overlooking the shore. And there he was, still leaning against the hood like something straight out of one of the old James Dean movies her grandma watched. All bad boy, bad attitude that just screamed "reform me."

Sarah's stomach rolled faster than the waves. They shared the same homeroom teacher, but he hadn't seemed to know she existed other than passing her a lunch tray on pizza day two months ago.

Breathless, she slowed a few feet away and tried to look casual as she walked up to his car. "What are you doing here?"

"Giving you a ride home from work." He stared right back, unsmiling, his blue eyes locked on her face until her hand gravitated upward to check for stray hairs slipping out of her ponytail.

And then it hit her. He was here for her. Oh. God.

The palm trees rustled and the waves crashed while she searched for something cool to say back when she really wanted to break out a quick happy dance barefoot on the sand.

She trailed her fingers along the hood of his car. "What if I'd worked for another two hours?"

"Why are you out here then?"

Um, well, she would have to admit to coming outside just for him. "What if I already have a ride?"

"Fine then, I'll leave." He turned away.

"Wait. Don't go." She clasped his arm.

Sheetrock-hard muscles flexed under her fingertips. His skin was so hot it sent tingles up her hand, then showering throughout her whole body. Wow. Just... Wow.

She let go slowly, fingers curling into a fist to hold on to the feeling a little longer. "My feet hurt and I'd rather not wait for my grandmother. My parents' second car has a busted transmission. So yes, thank you. I'll accept with a smile."

"Good." He nodded, slowly pushing away from his car. "I enjoy it when you smile, Sarah."

And she enjoyed the way he said her name, low and rumbly, like the way distant thunder carried softly over the water. "I need to call my grandma and let her know she doesn't have to come get me. She'll be happy to turn in early, actually."

"Okay then."

Backing up for as long as she could without stumbling, she finally turned, running up to use a payphone by the tennis courts. If she went into the restaurant, her boss might figure out she wasn't sick.

She stuffed down the twinge of guilt over the lost work hours—the lost wages. Her parents needed the money now more than ever since their second car finally gasped its last breath and went to that big car lot in the sky. They were all crossing their fingers that her dad's truck would last long enough for them to save up for a replacement for her mom's hatchback.

God, it was selfish of her to punch out early just to spend time with Rafe Cameron, to act like the carefree high school girl she couldn't afford to be. Still, she couldn't make herself stop. There was something about Rafe that tugged at her, a maturity and focus in his eyes she didn't see in the other boys.

Five minutes later, she'd called Grandma Kat—and lied about who was driving her home after work since her grandmother always referred to him as that wild Cameron boy. Sarah didn't agree. In her opinion, Rafe was more of a loner, a nonconformist.

But she would deal with her grandmother's worries later. Right now, she was sitting in the passenger seat of Rafe Cameron's El Camino and her family thought she was still at work.

For two more hours.

The scent of the ocean and surfboard oil drifted in through the window and she wondered when he found time for the beach. He worked more hours than she did. His tool belt bounced lightly on the bench seat between them with the occasional thunk and rattle of wrenches colliding.

"Thanks for the ride." She couldn't resist asking, "What made you decide to pick me up?"

"I saw you walking home alone last night." The dashboard lights illuminated the hard line of his jaw as he stared out at the two-lane coastline road. "It's not safe."

"My grandmother said the same thing, which was why she was coming to get me." Grandma Kat had been mad, really mad when she figured out Sarah had walked home on her own, and Kathleen Richards didn't get angry often. All the more reason to keep this drive a secret. "My parents work the night shift at Worth Industries and I hate to put other people out. It's not that far to walk if I catch the bus. And Vista del Mar isn't exactly inner-city crime central even in the summer." More of a sedate seaside town, just north of San Diego if she needed a big-city experience. Which she didn't.

She'd lived in Vista del Mar all her life and couldn't imagine anywhere else she would ever want to be other than here with her family and the beach. A beach she didn't get to see nearly enough of lately.

"Rafe, would you mind if we drove around for a while? I've been cooped up inside all day and I could really use the fresh air."

"On one condition."

Her stomach knotted as she thought of her grandmother's warnings about Rafe's wild reputation as a rule breaker. "What would that be?"

"Smile. Remember? I really like seeing you happy."

Relief flooded through her and before she realized what had happened, she was grinning. She threw caution off faster than she whipped her confining hair tie from her ponytail.

Rafe just nodded and floored the gas pedal down the shoreline road.

* * *

Rafe steered his beat-up, piece-of-crap El Camino along the seaside road toward the highest bluff, Busted Bluff. People went there to make out, but the spot was his favorite for another reason. From there, he could look over Vista del Mar and imagine getting out of this dead-end town.

He had plans.

So what was he doing here, tonight with Sarah Richards? Hell if he understood. He only knew that all day long he hadn't been able to shake the image of her walking home alone last night. He'd followed her the whole way to her house to make sure she got inside safely.

Then he'd realized she never noticed him trailing her. That scared the hell out of him. What if he'd been a perv or murderer? He could have followed her right off the street and no one would have noticed.

His gut knotted.

Now here he was. Giving her a ride with gas he couldn't afford and a deep, deep need to watch the way her red hair whipped in the wind. To find out if the lip gloss she wore was flavored, to find out what she tasted like.

To see Sarah smile again.

Crap. This was a stupid idea.

She shifted in her seat, elbow hooked out the open window. The gusting breeze teased open the neck of her shirt, revealing a hint of curves and lace. His body tightened. No surprise. He'd been attracted to her since the first day of ninth grade when she came back from summer break with breasts.

Really bad idea, Cameron.

Sarah reached for the radio.

He stopped with a touch to the wrist. "It doesn't work."

Her gaze snapped straight to his, her eyes wide. Aware.

"Oh, okay." Her hand fell away. "I just thought some music would fill the silence. You don't talk much."

Tearing his gaze off her and back to the road, he hooked

his hand over the steering wheel. The feel of her soft skin still burned his fingers. "How about you do the talking for me?"

Good thing the January night wasn't too cool or too hot, because his heater and A/C had long ago died, too, and a replacement was outside his budget.

"I'd like that. To talk to you, I mean." She scraped her long hair from her face. "We, uh, don't have to go straight to my house. Grandma Kat isn't expecting me to check in for a while."

Alarms jangled in his head again. "Do you think it was smart to tell me that? Nobody's expecting you and nobody knows who you're with."

"What makes you think no one knows I'm with you?"

He just looked at her.

"Okay, right." She scrunched her nose. "My parents would be…upset that I'm riding with you rather than at work or at home studying."

He should probably tell her to opt for studying next time and stay away from him. His father had brought him up to believe a real man protected women. Except in the end there hadn't been anything they could do for his mom.

His fists tightened around the steering wheel. "You should be more careful."

"Like not walking home alone. I get it." She rolled her eyes with her signature redheaded spunk he silently applauded. "Are you here to give me a ride or a lecture?"

"Both, if you need them."

That hushed her up, but not for long, he would bet. Sarah Richards always had something to say, an observation, an opinion. She never let anyone or anything get her down, and he liked that about her. So he waited…

She drummed her fingers on the seat between them. Close. But not touching. "Eighteen years in the same town, twelve grades in the same schools and this is the first time we've really talked. How strange is that?"

"We've talked, twice, as a matter of fact."

"Hah," she laughed once and shook her head. "You mean in the second grade when I fell off the monkey bars and you said, 'Get up and quit crying, you big baby'? I hardly think that counts as a conversation. Especially since my wrist was broken. You're lucky I didn't punch you."

He remembered the day well. How freaked he'd been seeing her hurt. After school, he'd beat up that little snot Quentin Dobbs, who'd shoved her off the monkey bars. "I made you quit thinking about the broken wrist for a while."

"Hmmm... I hadn't thought of it that way. Fair enough. You get double conversation points for that one. And what about the other conversation? Passing me a lunch tray doesn't count, by the way."

He hadn't meant to bring up the other time. Since she already knew the answer anyway, he said, "When we were fifteen, you spoke to me at my mother's funeral."

Her fingers stopped drumming. The air went still as he remembered that day. She'd squeezed his hand, tucking a tissue into his fist so no one would see. Her heart was too damn big for a world where people took advantage of anyone who wasn't always checking their back. His chest went tight.

Sarah ducked her face into his line of sight. "I'm surprised you remember anything from that day. I can't imagine a world without my mom or dad, or even my grandma."

Rafe stared unblinking at road leading up to the bluff. He'd spent a lot of hours there looking out over Vista del Mar, getting a bird's-eye view of the vast gap between the haves and the have-nots. Lights burned from inside thousands of little stucco houses crammed together. Then a handful of mansions glowed in large, exclusive lots on the beach. The Worth mansion, the largest of all, was lit up like a football field.

Deep in his gut, he knew he would own one of those waterfront estates someday. And he would always regret that he couldn't have given his mother that favorite view of hers to look out over one last time.

His chest went tighter. "Can we talk about something else? I shouldn't have even brought it up."

"Of course. I'm sorry." She settled back into her seat.

Sarah Richards was too nice. He should turn the car around and take her straight home. He didn't need to complicate his life, especially not now, so close to graduation. So close to kicking off his plans, to make something of himself, to pay his mother back for all the sacrifices she made for him. Sacrifices that cost her life.

And yet, as he pulled the car to a stop on top of Busted Bluff, he couldn't keep the words from falling out of his mouth. "Want to sit in the back of the truck and check out the stars?"

Sitting on a worn-soft quilt in the back of Rafe's El Camino, Sarah hugged her knees to her chest. Vista del Mar twinkled in the night, half-awake, half-asleep. Not in some big-city way, though, but lights from houses and families. A breeze blew in off the ocean, lifting her hair and teasing her nose with the sea-salty scent she'd been craving all day.

Wearing a jean jacket as the temperature dropped, Rafe settled beside her. He carried two cans in his hand, labels eclipsed by his big grip.

Unease skittered up her spine. She scooted away, the blanket snagging on the rusty rasp of metal. "Um, no thank you. I don't drink."

Chuckling softly, he set the can beside her. A Dr Pepper.

"Oh, sorry." She felt the flush heat her skin. "I didn't mean to judge you."

He rolled the soda can between his palms. "I don't have the luxury of getting busted for a DUI. My dad can't afford some rich lawyer to get the case thrown out on a technicality."

"Maybe in that sense being poor isn't such a bad thing—" she popped open the can "—when it teaches us to be responsible for our own actions."

He pinned her with a piercing blue stare. "Is that what you tell yourself when you're walking home alone in the dark because your parents can't afford to get a busted transmission fixed? Did I get that guess right?"

"Negativity breeds more negativity." She sipped her soda to avoid sinking too deep, too fast into his amazing eyes.

"Okay then, how about this?" Hand still holding his soda, he gestured to the city skyline as if toasting Vista del Mar. "I'm going to own this town one day."

Such a deep conviction rang in his voice she could almost believe something so outrageous was possible. "I imagine Mr. Worth won't like that much."

"I imagine he won't." His Dr Pepper can pinged and dented under his tightening fist. "He'll just have to get over it."

Rafe made no secret of how much he resented the town mogul. How he blamed Ronald Worth for his mother's death from COPD, insisting particulates from the factory killed her. Sarah shivered. It scared her to think the plant might not be up to the right codes. Her parents worked there, after all. Her grandmother was Mr. Worth's personal assistant. He might be a tough businessman, but she couldn't bring herself to believe he could be downright dishonest. Evil even.

Maybe if Rafe could see a different side to Mr. Worth, see the person underneath the wealth, then he could find some peace about his mother's tragic death.

"Mr. Worth was in the restaurant tonight with his daughter, Emma," she said carefully, watching his eyes for any sign of impending explosion. "They were so quiet through their whole meal, and they both kept looking at the empty chairs. Her brother's in boarding school now, and her mom... Well, you understand how tough it is for Emma right now, getting over her mother's death."

His fist crushed the can. He flung it away so hard it thudded against a tree, then rolled off the edge of the bluff.

She touched his arm lightly. "I'm sorry. I didn't mean to upset you."

"You're right to feel sorry for the kid, losing her mom that way, then being stuck with a cold jerk for a father."

Okay, making him sympathize with Ronald Worth was a lost cause. Time to move on to safer territory before she sabotaged her time with Rafe.

"Tell me more about how you're going to buy up the town." She grinned at him, scrunching her nose. "I like it when you smile."

He raised one eyebrow at her repeat of his words. "Are you flirting with me?"

"Honestly?" She exhaled hard. "I'm too nervous to flirt."

"I make you nervous?" Leaning toward her, he flattened a hand just behind her. Close. Really close. "Good. I should."

She drew in his soap-fresh smell. Wanted to lean into him and find out what it felt like to have his mouth on hers.

What if she didn't have another chance? "And yet you prove yourself to be nice with all these warnings."

"But I have you here, parking with me." Each word brushed warm breath over her in an almost kiss.

"What do you intend to do about that?" she asked, she wanted…she dared.

Silently, he skimmed the back of his knuckles down her arm. Even with her shirt and sweater muting his touch, a tingle spread through her. All her nerve endings pulled tight and hot. He linked his fingers with hers and raised her hand.

Rafe pressed his lips against the racing pulse in her wrist, right over where she'd broken it in the second grade. "I'm sorry I wasn't nicer to you that day on the playground."

Her hand shook. God, all of her insides quivered from the feel of his mouth on her. "You're forgiven."

"Thanks, Sarah…." His smile caressed the sensitive inside of her wrist.

Then his hands stroked higher, up her arms until he cupped the back of her neck. Finally, thank goodness finally, his head dipped toward her, blocking out the moon and all of Vista del Mar until it was just her and him in their own little world.

He slanted his mouth against hers, more gently than she would have expected. He was such a guy of tough angles, attitude and even bitterness. But right now, she felt all the good in him she'd hoped—known—was there.

The stroke of his tongue along the seam of her lips was the only encouragement she needed. She locked her arms around his neck and committed her all to the kiss. She tested the glide of his hair through her fingers, mussing it the way she'd imagined doing so many times. This was the Rafe in her dreams, the man in her diary fantasies.

She'd told herself it was just a high-school crush. A really long-held high-school crush that only her grandmother had guessed. He wasn't her type. He wasn't even attainable, this brooding guy who only went out with girls who dressed all in black.

But she didn't want to think about the other people he'd dated. She didn't want to think about her grandmother's warnings to set her sights on another boy.

Tonight, Rafe was here with her. Kissing her. Stroking up and down her back in a way that sent goose bumps prickling along her skin. Making her ache to press closer and demand more from the kiss, from the moment, from him.

The buttons of his jean jacket pressed into her flesh as she burrowed closer. Her hands parted his coat and twisted in his T-shirt.

And then suddenly cool air was rushing between them. Rafe had pulled away. His chest pumped fast, his hand heavy on her shoulder. It was like he was keeping distance between them, but couldn't totally let her go.

She struggled to get her bearings, but the lights of Vista del Mar swirled on the horizon. She loosened her hold on his T-shirt and smoothed the wrinkles she put in the body-warmed cotton.

Oh, my. Muscles.

His low growl of pleasure rumbled under her fingertips. Her nails dug in lightly.

"Ah, kitten, this isn't smart," he said softly, hauling her against his chest anyway.

He was breathing every bit as fast as she was. His heart hammered under her ear. She swallowed hard against the kick of relief. The crazy way she felt wasn't one-sided. He wanted her, too.

She might be reckless for coming here with him. Her grandmother would chew her out, lecturing her into infinity if she found out.

But she couldn't ignore the hopeful voice whispering in her head that maybe all her late-night fantasies about Rafe, about them together, could come true. Sure they were young, but she knew deep inside they were meant to be together. She could help him follow those dreams, be by his side every step of the way.

She understood all the hard work that went into making it in this town. God, did she ever understand. He needed her, whether he realized it or not.

So for his sake as well as her own, she was here. If it all worked out for her and Rafe, then the risk would have been well worth taking.

And if it didn't?

She refused to think that way. Tonight was the start of a future with Rafe and she wouldn't let anything stand in her way with keeping him right here in her arms.

* * * * *

COMING NEXT MONTH

Available February 8, 2011

#2065 THE BILLIONAIRE GETS HIS WAY
Elizabeth Bevarly

#2066 SEDUCED: THE UNEXPECTED VIRGIN
Emily McKay
The Takeover

#2067 THE BOSS'S BABY AFFAIR
Tessa Radley
Billionaires and Babies

#2068 TAMING THE VIP PLAYBOY
Katherine Garbera
Miami Nights

#2069 TO TEMPT A SHEIKH
Olivia Gates
Pride of Zohayd

#2070 MILLION-DOLLAR AMNESIA SCANDAL
Rachel Bailey

Try these Healthy and Delicious Spring Rolls!

INGREDIENTS

2 packages rice-paper spring roll wrappers (20 wrappers)

1 cup grated carrot

¼ cup bean sprouts

1 cucumber, julienned

1 red bell pepper, without stem and seeds, julienned

4 green onions finely chopped— use only the green part

DIRECTIONS

1. Soak one rice-paper wrapper in a large bowl of hot water until softened.

2. Place a pinch each of carrots, sprouts, cucumber, bell pepper and green onion on the wrapper toward the bottom third of the rice paper.

3. Fold ends in and roll tightly to enclose filling.

4. Repeat with remaining wrappers. Chill before serving.

Find this and many more delectable recipes including the perfect dipping sauce in

YOUR BEST BODY NOW
by
TOSCA RENO
WITH STACY BAKER

Bestselling Author of
THE EAT-CLEAN DIET®

Available wherever books are sold!

NTRSERIESJAN